Hermann Hesse was born in Germany, at Calw, Württemberg, on 2 July 1877. He began his career as a bookseller and started to write and publish poetry at the age of twenty-one. Five years later he enjoyed his first major success with his novels on youth and educational problems: first *Peter Camenzind* (1904), then *The Prodigy* (1905), followed by *Gertrude* (1910), *Rosshalde* (1914), *Knulp* (1915), and *Demian* (1919). Later, when as a protest against German militarism in the First World War he settled permanently in Switzerland, he established himself as one of the greatest literary figures of the German-speaking world. Hesse's deep humanity and searching philosophy were further developed in such masterly novels as *Siddhartha* (1922), *Steppenwolf* (1927), and *Narziss and Goldmund* (1930), which together with his poems and a number of critical works won him a leading place among contemporary thinkers. In 1946 he won the Nobel Prize for Literature. Hermann Hesse died in 1962 shortly after his eighty-fifth birthday.

D0591976

By the same author

Peter Camenzind
The Prodigy
Gertrude
Rosshalde
Knulp
Strange News from Another Star
Klingsor's Last Summer
Wandering
Siddhartha
Steppenwolf
Narziss and Goldmund
The Journey to the East
The Glass Bead Game
If the War Goes On . . .
Poems
Autobiographical Writings
My Belief
Reflections
Crisis
Stories of Five Decades
A Pictorial Biography (illustrated non-fiction)

HERMANN HESSE

Demian

translated from the German by W. J. Strachan

GRAFTON BOOKS
A Division of the Collins Publishing Group

LONDON GLASGOW
TORONTO SYDNEY AUCKLAND

Grafton Books
A Division of the Collins Publishing Group
8 Grafton Street, London W1X 3LA

Published by Grafton Books 1969
Reprinted 1969, 1971 (twice), 1972 (three times), 1974,
1975, 1976, 1978 (twice), 1979, 1981, 1982, 1984, 1985,
1986

First published in Great Britain jointly by
Peter Owen Ltd and Vision Press Ltd 1960
Reprinted 1965

ISBN 0-586-02776-9

Printed and bound in Great Britain by
Collins, Glasgow

Set in Monotype Garamond

Demian

I cannot tell my story without going a long way back. If it were possible I would go back much farther still to the very earliest years of my childhood and beyond them to my family origins.

When poets write novels they are apt to behave as if they were gods, with the power to look beyond and comprehend any human story and serve it up as if the Almighty Himself, omnipresent, were relating it in all its naked truth. That I am no more able to do than the poets. But my story is more important to me than any poet's story to him, for it is my own – and it is the story of a human being – not an invented, idealised person but a real, live, unique being. What constitutes a real, live human being is more of a mystery than ever these days, and men – each one of whom is a valuable, unique experiment on the part of nature – are shot down wholesale. If, however, we were not something more than unique human beings and each man jack of us could really be dismissed from this world with a bullet, there would be no more point in relating stories at all. But every man is not only himself; he is also the unique, particular, always significant and remarkable point where the phenomena of the world intersect once and for all and never again. That is why every man's story is important, eternal, sacred; and why every man while he lives and fulfils the will of nature is a wonderful creature, deserving the utmost attention. In each individual the spirit is made flesh, in each one the whole of creation suffers, in each one a Saviour is crucified.

Few people nowadays know what man is. Many feel it intuitively and die more easily for that reason, just as I shall die more easily when I have completed this story.

I cannot call myself a scholar. I have always been and still am a seeker but I no longer do my seeking among the stars or in books. I am beginning to hear the lessons which whisper in my blood. Mine is not a pleasant story, it does not possess the gentle harmony of invented tales; like the lives of all men who have given up trying to deceive themselves, it is a mixture of nonsense and chaos, madness and dreams.

The life of every man is a way to himself, an attempt at a way, the suggestion of a path. No man has ever been utterly himself, yet every man strives to be so, the dull, the intelligent, each one as best he can. Each man to the end of his days carries round with him vestiges of his birth – the slime and egg-shells of the primeval world. There are many who never become human; they remain frogs, lizards, ants. Many men are human beings above and fish below. Yet each one represents an attempt on the part of nature to create a human being. We enjoy a common origin in our mothers; we all come from the same pit. But each individual, who is himself an experimental throw from the depths, strives towards his own goal. We can understand each other; but each person is able to interpret himself to himself alone.

Two Worlds

I begin my story with an event from the time when I was ten years old, attending the local grammar school in our small country town.

I can still catch the fragrance of many things which stir me with feelings of melancholy and send delicious shivers of delight through me – dark and sunlit streets, houses and towers, clock chimes and people's faces, rooms full of comfort and warm hospitality, rooms full of secret and profound, ghostly fears. It is a world that savours of warm corners, rabbits, servant girls, household remedies and dried fruit. It was the meeting-place of two worlds; day and night came thither from two opposite poles.

There was the world of my parents' house, or rather it was even more circumscribed and embraced only my parents themselves. This world was familiar to me in almost every aspect – it meant mother and father, love and severity, model behaviour and school. It was a world of quiet brilliance, clarity and cleanliness; in it gentle and friendly conversation, washed hands, clean clothes and good manners were the order of the day. In this world the morning hymn was sung, Christmas celebrated. Through it ran straight lines and paths that led into the future; here were duty and guilt, bad conscience and confessions, forgiveness and good resolutions, love and reverence, wisdom and Bible readings. In this world you had to conduct yourself so that life should be pure, unsullied, beautiful and well-ordered.

The other world, however, also began in the middle of our own house and was completely different; it smelt different, spoke a different language, made different claims and promises. This second world was peopled with servant girls and workmen, ghost stories and scandalous rumours, a gay tide of monstrous, intriguing, frightful, mysterious things; it included the slaughterhouse and the prison, drunken and scolding women, cows in labour, foundered horses, tales of housebreaking, murder and suicide. All these attractive and hideous, wild and cruel things were on every side, in the next street, the neighbouring house. Policemen and tramps moved about in it, drunkards beat their wives, bunches of young women poured out of the factories in the evening, old women could put a spell on you and make you ill; thieves lived in the wood; incendiaries were caught by mounted gendarmes. Everywhere you could smell this vigorous, second world – everywhere, that is, except in our house where my mother and father lived. There it was all goodness. It was wonderful to be living in a house in a reign of peace, order, tranquillity, duty and good conscience, forgiveness and love – but it was no less wonderful to know there was the other, the loud and shrill, sullen and violent world from which you could dart back to your mother in one leap.

The odd thing about it was that these worlds should border on each other so closely. When, for example, our servant Lina sat by the door in the living-room at evening prayers and joined in the hymn in her clear voice, her freshly washed hands folded on her smoothed down pinafore, she belonged wholly and utterly to mother and father, to us, the world of light and righteousness. But when in the kitchen or woodshed immediately afterwards she told me the story of the little headless man or started bickering with her neighbours in the little butcher's shop, she became a different person, belonged to another world and was veiled in mystery. And it was the same with everybody, most of all with myself. Doubtless I was part of the world of light and righteousness as the child of my parents, but wherever I listened or directed my gaze I found the other thing and I lived half in the other world, although it was often strangely alien to me and I inevitably suffered from panic and a bad conscience. Indeed at times I preferred life in the forbidden world and my return to the world of light – necessary and worthy though it might be – was often almost like a return to something less attractive, something both more drab and tedious. I was often conscious that my destiny in life was to become like my father and mother; pure, righteous and disciplined; but that was a long way ahead; first one had to sit studying at school, do tests and examinations, and the way always led through and past the other, dark world and it was not impossible that one might remain permanently in it. I had read, with passionate interest, stories of prodigal sons to whom this had happened. There was always the return to their father and the path of righteousness that was so fine and redeeming that I felt convinced that this alone was the right, good, worthy thing; and yet I found the part of the story which was played among the wicked and lost souls far more alluring. If it had been permissible to speak out and confess, I should have admitted that it often seemed a shame to me that the Prodigal Son should atone and be 'found' again – though this feeling was only vaguely present deep down within me like a presentiment or possibility. When I pictured the devil to myself, I found no difficulty in visualizing him in the street below, disguised or undisguised, or at the fair or in a tavern but never at home.

My sisters belonged likewise to the world of light. It often seemed to me that they were closer in temperament to father and mother, better and more refined and with fewer faults than I. Of course they had their defects and their vagaries but these did not appear to me to go very deep. It was not as with me whose contact with evil could become so oppressive and painful and to whom the dark world lay so much closer. My sisters, like my parents, were to be spared and respected, and if one quarrelled with them one always felt in the wrong afterwards; as if one were the instigator, who must crave forgiveness. For in offending my sisters, I was offending my parents, which made me guilty of a breach of good conduct. There were secrets that I would have been less reluctant to tell the most reprobate street urchin than my sisters. On good days when everything seemed light and my conscience in good order, I enjoyed playing with them, being good and kind to them and seeing myself sharing their aura of nobility. It was like a foretaste of being an angel! That was the highest thing we could conceive of and we thought it would be sweet and wonderful to be angels, surrounded with sweet music and fragrance reminiscent of Christmas and happiness. How rarely did such hours and days come along! I would often be engaged in some harmless and authorized game which became too exciting and vigorous for my sisters and led to squabbles and misery, and when I lost my temper I was terrible and did and said things that seemed so depraved to me that they seared my heart even as I was in the act of doing and saying them. These occasions were followed by gloomy hours of sorrow and penitence and the painful moment when I begged forgiveness and then, once again, a beam of light, a tranquil, grateful unclouded goodness for hours – or moments as the case might be.

I attended the local grammar school. The mayor's son and the head forester's son were in my class and sometimes joined me. They were wild fellows, yet they belonged to the 'respectable' world. But I also had close relations with neighbours' sons, village lads on whom we normally looked down. It is with one of these that my story begins.

One half-holiday – I was little more than ten years old – I was playing around with two boys from the neighbourhood. A bigger boy joined us, a rough, burly lad of about thirteen from the village school, the tailor's son. His father drank, and the whole family had a bad name.

I knew Franz Kromer well, and went about in fear of him so that I felt very uneasy when he came along. He had already acquired grown-up ways and imitated the walk and speech of the young factory workers. With him as ringleader we climbed down the river bank near the bridge and hid ourselves away from the world under the first arch. The narrow strip between the vaulted bridge and the lazily flowing river consisted of nothing but general rubbish and broken pots, tangles of rusty barbed wire and similar jetsam. Occasionally we came across things we could make use of. We had to comb these stretches of bank under Franz Kromer's orders and show him our discoveries. These he either kept himself or threw into the water. We were told to notice whether there were any items made of lead, brass or tin. He retained these together with an old comb made of horn. I was very uncomfortable in his presence, not because I knew my father would forbid this relationship but out of fear of Franz himself, but I was grateful for being included, and treated like the others. He gave the orders and we obeyed as if it was an old custom, although it was my first time.

At length we sat down on the ground; Franz spat into the water and looked like a grown-up; he spat through a gap between his teeth and scored a hit wherever he aimed. A conversation started and the boys boasted about their grand deeds and beastly tricks. I remained silent and yet feared to offend by my silence and incur Kromer's wrath. Both my comrades had made up to him, and avoided me from the start. I was a stranger among them and felt that my clothes and manners were taken as a kind of challenge. Franz could not possibly have any love for me, a grammar school boy and a gentleman's son and I was in no doubt that the other two, if it came to it, would disown and desert me.

Finally, out of sheer nervousness, I began to talk. I invented a long story of robbery, in which I featured as the hero. One night in the corner by the mill a friend and I had stolen a whole sackful of apples, not just ordinary apples but pippins, golden pippins of the best kind at that. I was taking refuge in my story from the dangers of the moment and found no difficulty in inventing and relating it. In order not to dry up too soon and perhaps become involved in something worse, I gave full rein to my narrative powers. One of us, I reported, had always stood guard while the other sat in the tree and chucked the apples down, and the sack had got so heavy that in the end we had to open it and leave half behind, but we came back half an hour later and fetched them too.

I hoped for some applause at the end of my story; I had warmed up to the narrative at last, carried away by my own eloquence. The two smaller boys were silent, waiting, but Franz Kromer gave me a penetrating look through his narrowed eyes. "Is that yarn true?" he asked in a menacing tone.

"Yes," I said.

"Really and truly?"

"Yes, really and truly," I asserted defiantly while I choked inwardly with fear.

"Can you swear to it?"

I was very afraid but I said 'Yes' without hesitation.

"Hand on your heart?"

"Hand on my heart."

"Right then," he said and turned away.

I thought this was all very satisfactory and I was glad when he got up and turned to go home. When we were on the bridge I ventured timidly that I must go home.

"No desperate hurry," Franz laughed. "We go the same way."

He sauntered along slowly and I did not dare to go ahead, but he was in fact going in the direction of our house. When we arrived, and I saw our front door and the fat doorknocker, the sun in the windows and the curtains in my mother's room, I breathed a sigh of relief. Back home! O good, blessed home – coming back to the world of light and peace!

When I had quickly opened the door and slipped in ready to slam it behind me, Franz Kromer edged in too. In the cool, gloomy paved passage which was lit solely from the courtyard he stood close to me and said in a low voice, "No hurry, you!"

I looked at him terrified. His grip on my arm was like a vice. I tried to guess what was going on in his mind and whether he was going to do me some mischief. If I were to let out a loud and vigorous shriek would some one above be quick enough to save me? But I gave up the idea.

"What is it?" I asked, "what do you want?"

"Oh, nothing much, I merely wanted to ask you something. The others needn't hear."

"Well? What do you want me to tell you? I must go up, you know."

"I suppose you know who owns the orchard by the corner mill?"

"No, I don't. The miller I think."

Franz had put his arm round me and drawn me close to him so that I couldn't avoid looking into his face at close range. He had an evil gleam in his eyes and he gave an ugly laugh. His face was full of cruelty and sense of power.

"Yes, kid, I can tell you who owns the orchard. I've known for a long time that people have been stealing apples and I also know that the man in question said he would give two marks reward to anyone who could tell him who stole the fruit."

"Heavens!" I exclaimed. "But you wouldn't let on to him?"

I felt that it would be futile to appeal to his sense of honour. He belonged to the 'other' world; betrayal was no crime as far as he was concerned. That much was clear to me. The people of the 'other' world were not like us in these matters.

"Not let on! My dear fellow, do you think I can mint my own money and produce a couple of marks out of a hat? I'm poor. I haven't a rich father like you and if I can earn two marks I've got to earn them. He might even give me more."

He suddenly left me. Our house passage no longer smelt of peace and safety; the world was tumbling about my ears. He would denounce me as a criminal; they would inform my father, perhaps the police would come. All the horror of chaos threatened me; the outlook for me was horrible and dangerous. The fact that I had not committed a theft was a mere detail. I had sworn that I had. God in heaven! Tears welled in my eyes. I felt that I should have to buy myself out and I groped desperately. Not an apple, not a pen-knife; nothing. Then I remembered my watch. It was a silver watch but it did not go. I just wore it 'like that.' It came to me from my grandmother. I quickly drew it out.

"Kromer," I said, "You mustn't tell; it would be a beastly thing to do. Look, I'll give you my watch; unluckily it's the only thing I have, but you can have it. It's made of silver," I added nervously. "It's good workmanship and it's only got some slight defect which can easily be put right."

He smiled and took the watch in his large hand. I looked at that hand and felt how rough and hostile it was towards me and how it was trying to tighten its grip on my life and peace of mind.

"It's silver," I repeated nervously.

"I don't give a damn for your silver and your old watch!" he said with withering scorn. "Get it repaired yourself!"

"But Franz," I exclaimed, trembling with fear lest he walk off. "Just wait a moment! Take the watch! It really is made of silver, honestly. And I haven't got anything else."

He gave me a cold, scornful look.

"Well, you know who I'm going to see. Or I might even inform the police. The sergeant is a friend of mine."

He turned as if to go. I held him back by his coat sleeve. He must not go. I would much rather die than have to suffer what would happen if he went off like that.

"Franz," I implored, hot with emotion, "don't do anything stupid! It *is* a joke, isn't it?"

"It's a joke all right, but it might be an expensive one for you."

"Just tell me Franz, what I am to do and I'll do whatever you like!"

His eyes narrowed and he laughed again.

"Don't be a fool!" he said with false good humour. "You know as well as I do. I can earn two marks and I'm not rich; you know I can't afford to chuck them away. But you're rich; you've got a watch. You've only got to give me two marks and everything will be all right."

I grasped his logic. But two marks! It was far away beyond my means and as unattainable as ten, a hundred, a thousand marks. I did not have any money. There was a money-box which mother kept for me and it contained a few ten and five pfennig pieces put in by uncles when they came to visit us and by other family friends on similar occasions. Apart from that I had nothing. I was not given any pocket money at that age.

"I haven't got anything, honestly," I said gloomily. "I haven't any money. But I'll give you anything else. I've got a book about Indians and soldiers and a compass. I'll fetch it for you."

Kromer merely contracted his lips in an evil sneer and spat on the ground.

"Talk sense!" he commanded. "You can keep your stupid rubbish. A compass! Don't make me angry, do you hear, and hand over the money!"

"But I haven't any. They don't give me any. I can't do anything about it!"

"Bring me two marks tomorrow morning then. I'll wait for them downstairs after school. See you have them ready, or you'll find out what happens if you don't."

"Yes, but where am I going to get them from when I haven't got any?"

"There's plenty of money in your house. That's up to you. Tomorrow after school then. And I tell you ... if you don't bring it ..." he flashed an intimidating glance at me, spat again and vanished like a shadow.

I felt unable to go upstairs. My life was wrecked. I thought vaguely of running away and never returning or of drowning myself. I sat down in the dark on the bottom step of our outside staircase, withdrew into myself and abandoned myself to my misery. Lina found me there weeping when she came down with a basket to collect some firewood.

I begged her to say nothing about it, and went upstairs. On the right of the glazed door hung father's hat and mother's sunshade; an atmosphere of homeliness and affection hung about all these things; my heart warmed to them gratefully as that of the Prodigal Son must have done when he was confronted with the sight and smell of the old familiar rooms of his house. But none of this was mine any longer; it all belonged to the world of my parents and I was deeply and guiltily engulfed in the alien tide. I was involved in excitement and wrong-doing, threatened by the enemy, beset by dangers, fear and scandal. The hat and the sunshade, the good old sandstone floor, the large picture over the hall cupboard and the voices of my elder sisters coming from the living-room, it was all more moving and precious than ever but it had ceased to be a comfort and something I could rely on and had become a kind of reproach. This was no longer my world; I could have no part in its cheerfulness and peace. My feet were defiled; I could not wipe them on the mat; I was accompanied by shadows of which this world of home knew nothing. I had had plenty of secrets, plenty of scares before but it had all been light-hearted compared to what I was bringing back with me that day. Fate was tracking me down, hands were reaching for me from which my mother could not protect me; of which she knew nothing. What my crime was – theft or lying – (had I not sworn a false oath by God and everything that was sacred?) – did not come into it. My sin was not this or that; my sin was that I was in league with the Devil. Why had I associated with him? Why had I listened to Kromer more than I had ever done to my father? Why had I lied about that theft, fathered myself with crime as if it had been a heroic deed? And now the Devil held me in his clutches, the enemy was at my shoulder.

For the time being my fear was not of the next day, it was the horrible certainty that I was treading the downhill path that led into darkness. I felt that my first lapse was bound to be followed by others and that my presence among my brothers and sisters, my demonstrations of affection towards my parents were a lie, that I was living a fate and a lie that I was hiding from them.

For a moment a flash of confidence and hope lit inside me as I stood looking at my father's hat. I would tell him the whole story, the judgement he passed and the punishment he meted out would make him into my confidant and saviour. It would only mean the kind of penance I had done often enough, a difficult and painful hour, a difficult and rueful request for forgiveness.

How sweet it all sounded. How tempting it was! But it was no use. I knew that I would not do it. I knew that I now had a secret, a debt which I had to work out for myself. Perhaps I was at the parting of the ways, perhaps from now on I would always belong to the wicked, depend on them, obey them, become one of their number. I had played the man and hero and now I must bear the consequences.

I was glad that my father upbraided me about my muddy shoes. It side-stepped the issue, the graver sin passed unnoticed and I got away with a reproach which I secretly transferred to the other affair. In so doing, a strange new feeling lit up inside me, an unpleasant, ruthless feeling, full of barbs – I felt superior to my father! For the moment I despised his ignorance; his reprimand about the muddy boots seemed trivial. "If you only knew," I thought, and felt like the criminal who is being tried for stealing a loaf of bread when he has confessed to a murder. It was an odious, hostile feeling but it was strong and it somehow fascinated me and took a firmer hold of me than any other aspect of my secret and my guilt. Perhaps, I thought, Kromer has already gone to the police and denounced me and while I am being treated here as a small child, storms are gathering above my head!

This was the all-important and permanent element in the whole experience as I have related it. It was the first crack in the sacrosanct person of my father, a first incision in the pillar on which my whole childhood's life had rested but which every man must destroy before he can become his own true self. The real, inner line of our fate consists of these experiences which are hidden from other people. A gash or wound of this kind grows together again; it is healed and forgotten, but in the inner recesses of our minds it lives on and bleeds.

I was so horrified by this new feeling that I would willingly have fallen at my father's feet and begged forgiveness. But you cannot crave forgiveness for anything fundamental and a child is as deeply aware of that as any wise man.

I felt the need to reflect on my problem and plan out my

course for the next day; but I failed completely. It was as much as I could do the whole evening to try and acclimatise myself to the different atmosphere in our sitting-room. Wall-clock and table, Bible and mirror, bookshelf and pictures were likewise leaving me behind, and I had to gaze at them with a frozen heart as I saw my world, my good, happy life becoming a thing of the past and breaking away from me. There was no escaping the fact that new tap-roots held me firmly anchored in a dark and alien land. For the first time in my life I was tasting death, and death tastes bitter – for it is birth pangs, fear and dread before some terrible renewal.

I was relieved when at length I found myself in bed. Just before, as a final torment, I had been subjected to family prayers and we had sung one of my favourite hymns. But I could not join in; every note was gall and bitterness. Nor could I join in the prayers when my father pronounced the blessing, and when he ended "God keep us all . . ." I felt rejected from the family circle. The grace of God was with them but not with me. I went up, cold and exhausted.

When I had lain in bed for a while in warmth and comfort, my heart once more turned back in fear and hovered in a panic round the events of the day. Mother had said her usual good-night, her step still sounded in the room, her candle still glowed through a chink in the door. Now I thought, she is coming back – she has guessed – and she will give me a good-night kiss and question me sympathetically about it all and then I can cry and the lump in my throat will melt and then I'll hug her and tell everything and it will be all right again and I shall be saved. After the chink in the door had become dark again, I listened for a while, feeling that it must and would happen.

Then my mind went back to the incident and I seemed to be looking my enemy in the face. I could see him clearly; he had screwed up one eye and his lips were twisted in a leer. And even as I watched, I was consumed by the inescapable truth and he became bigger and uglier and a fiendish glint lit up his eye. He stood close beside me until I fell asleep but then I dreamed not of him and the day that was over but that we were travelling in a boat, my parents, my sisters and myself and we were surrounded by the peaceful and heightened glow of a day's holiday. I woke up in the middle of the night still conscious of the after-taste of that blessedness and my sisters' white summer-dresses still shining in the sun when I fell from Paradise back into reality and once more stood face to face with the enemy with the 'evil eye.'

Next day when mother came hurrying up and called out that it was late and asked why I was still in bed, I must have looked ill and when she asked if anything was the matter with me, I had a fit of vomiting.

It was something gained. It was wonderful to be slightly ill and allowed to lie in bed and drink camomile tea and listen to mother tidying up in the next room and Lina dealing with the butcher in the hall outside. A morning off from school was something magic and fairylike, the sun played in the room but it was not the same sun they shut out with the green curtains at school. But even that I could not enjoy today; it had a false ring about it.

If I could only die! But, as on so many occasions, I was only slightly ill and nothing happened. It saved me from school but not from Kromer who was waiting for me in the market place at eleven o'clock. And my mother's amiability brought me no comfort; it was heavy and distressing. I pretended to be asleep while I pondered over it all again. It was no use; I had to be at the market at eleven o'clock. So I got up quietly at ten and said that I was feeling better. It meant, as usual in such cases, that I must either go to bed again or return to school in the afternoon. I said that I wanted to go to school. I had made a plan.

I could not go to Kromer empty-handed. I must get

hold of the little money-box that belonged to me. I knew there was not nearly enough money in it; but it was something and I felt that something was better than nothing and that Kromer at all costs must be appeased.

I felt guilty when I crept into my mother's room in my stockinged feet and took my money-box from her writing-table, but my conscience troubled me less than on the previous day. My heart beat so fast that I nearly suffocated and the situation was not improved when I discovered on first examining it at the bottom of the staircase that the box was locked. But it was not difficult to force; it was merely a matter of breaking a thin tinplate grid. I felt terrible about breaking it – I was committing a theft. Before this I had done nothing worse than pilfer lumps of sugar or fruit. But this was stealing although it was my own money. I realized defiantly that I was taking a step nearer to Kromer and his world and that it was so easy to go down bit by bit. The Devil might come for me now; there was no way back. I counted the money nervously; it had sounded so much in the box and was so painfully little in my hand. It came to sixty-five pfennig. I concealed the box on the ground floor, clasped the money in my hand and left the house without passing through the gateway. I thought I heard somebody upstairs shouting after me, but I hurried away.

There was still plenty of time; I crept off by roundabout ways through the alleys of a transformed town under clouds such as I had never seen before, past houses which stared at me and men who eyed me with suspicion. It occurred to me en route that one of my school-friends had once found a florin in the Cattle-Market. I wished I could pray that God might perform a miracle and allow me to make a similar find. But I had forfeited the right to pray. And in any case it would not have mended the box.

Franz Kromer spied me coming from a distance but he sauntered slowly towards me without appearing to notice me. When he was close, he beckoned me imperiously to follow him and went quickly on down the Strohgasse and across the road without once turning round until he finally stopped before a new building among the last houses. It had not yet been completed, the walls stood bare; there were no doors or windows. Kromer looked all around him and went in through the gap for the door, and I followed. He beckoned to me behind the wall and stretched out his hand.

"Have you got it?" he asked coldly.

I drew my clenched hand out of my pocket and emptied my money into his flat palm. He had counted it before the last five-pfennig piece had rattled out.

"There's sixty-five pfennig here," he said looking at me hard.

"Yes," I said nervously. "That's all I have; I know it's not enough. But it's all I have."

"I didn't think you were such a fool," he reproved, almost mildly, "things should be done right and proper between men of honour. I won't take anything from you that isn't correct, see. Take your nickel coins back, there! The other chap – you know who – doesn't try to beat me down. He pays up."

"But I haven't any more! It was my money-box."

"That's your affair. But I won't upset you. You can still owe me one mark thirty-five. When shall I get it?"

"Oh, you'll get it all right, Kromer. I can't quite say now – perhaps I'll have some more money tomorrow or the day after. You realize that I can't breathe a word to my father about this."

"That's nothing to do with me. I'm not one to do you harm. I could have my money by midday, you know, and I'm poor. You've got good clothes on and get better meals than me. But I won't say anything. I'm prepared to wait a bit. The day after tomorrow I'll give you a whistle at midday and then you can settle with me. You know my whistle?"

He let me hear it, though I had heard it often enough. "Yes," I said, "I know it."

He went off as if I had nothing to do with him. It had been a business transaction between us; nothing more.

I think Kromer's whistle would frighten me even to-day if I suddenly heard it. It seemed to me that I heard it, repeatedly. There was no place, game, work or thought which his whistle did not penetrate, the whistle which made me his slave and had become my fate. I frequently went into our small flower garden of which I was very fond on those mild, colourful autumn afternoons, and a strange urge prompted me to return to some of the games of my earlier boyhood. I was playing the part of someone younger than myself who was good, frank, innocent and secure, but in the midst of all this, always expected and yet horribly surprising and frightening, Kromer's whistle would sound from somewhere, interrupting my games and shattering my dreams. Then I had to go and follow my tormentor to odious places, render him an account and let myself be pressed for payment. The whole affair had probably not lasted more than a few weeks but to me they seemed years, an eternity. Only rarely was I able to produce an odd five-pfennig piece or a groschen stolen from the kitchen table when Lina had left the shopping-basket there. Each time I received a reprimand from Kromer who heaped scorn on my head; I was cheating him, trying to do him out of his rightful property. I was robbing him; making him miserable! Rarely have I felt so distressed in my life, never more desperate or so much in some one else's clutches. No one inquired about the money-box which I had filled with counters and restored to its place. But the scandal might break over my head any day. I was even more frightened of my mother when she crept quietly up to me than of Kromer's strident whistle – was she coming to ask about the box?

As I had appeared before my persecutor without money on many occasions, he began to find other means of torturing me. He made me work for him. He had to do various errands for his father which I had to do for him. Or he required me to execute some difficult feat – hop for ten minutes on one leg, attach a scrap of paper to the overcoat of some passer-by. These tortures continued many a night in my dreams as I lay in the sweat of a nightmare.

I began to feel ill. I kept having fits of sickness, and was easily chilled but at nights I sweated again. Mother suspected some hidden reason and showed me a great deal of sympathetic solicitude which only made me feel worse since I could not respond to her confidence.

One night she brought a piece of chocolate up to me when I was in bed. It was an echo of earlier years when I had often been vouchsafed similar little treats at night if I had been good. Now she stood there, holding out the chocolate. I felt so ill that I could only shake my head. She asked me what was the matter and stroked my hair. But I could only jerk out, "No, No! I don't want anything!" She deposited the chocolate on the bedside-table and left me. When she tried to find out the reason for my behaviour next day, I pretended not to understand. On one occasion she sent for the doctor who examined me and prescribed cold ablutions in the mornings.

My condition at that time was a kind of delirium. I lived in the midst of the ordered peace of our house, nervous and tormented like a ghost, with no part in the life of the others and rarely able to forget my troubles even for an hour. Towards my father who was often irritated and called me to account, I was cold and uncommunicative.

Salvation from my tormentor came from a totally un-
expected quarter, and at the same time I was conscious of
a new element in my life which has affected me right up
to the present day.

A new boy had just joined our school. He was the son
of a well-to-do widow who had come to live in our town
and he wore a mourning band on his sleeve. He was placed
in a higher class than mine and was several years older but
he soon impressed me as he impressed everybody else.
This remarkable boy seemed older than he looked; he did
not in fact seem like a boy at all. He moved among us more
childish members of the school strangely mature, like a
man, or rather a gentleman. He was not popular; he took
no part in games, still less in the general rough and tumble
and it was only the firm self-confident tone he adopted in
his attitude towards the masters that won him favour with
the other boys. He was called Max Demian.

One day, as happened now and again, an additional class
was put in our large classroom for one reason or another.
It was Demian's. We junior boys were having a scripture
lesson, the senior boys had to write an essay. While we were
being told the story of Cain and Abel, I kept glancing
over towards Demian whose face held a peculiar fascination for me, and I observed his bright, clever, unusually
resolute face bent diligently over his work; he looked less
like a schoolboy doing his 'prep.' than a research student
absorbed in some individual problem of his own. He did
not attract me; I was conscious, on the contrary, of a
certain antipathy between us; he was too self-possessed
and cool, too defiantly confident; his eyes had a grown-up
expression – which never commends them to young people

– faintly sad, with flashes of derision. But I could not help staring at him whether I liked him or not; hardly had he given me one glance, however, when I immediately averted my head in panic. When I think back to it to-day and how he looked as a schoolboy, I can certainly confirm that he was different from all the rest in every respect; an individual wholly in his own right, with his own personality stamped on him. Therefore – though he made every effort not to impress – he bore himself and behaved in every way like a prince moving about among peasants incognito and taking great pains to look like them.

He was walking behind me on the way home from school. When the others had run off, he caught me up and greeted me. Even his style of greeting, despite the fact that he imitated our schoolboy tone of voice, was grown-up and courteous.

"Shall we walk along together for a while?" he asked amiably. I was flattered and nodded. Then I described to him where I lived.

"Oh, there?" he smiled. "I know the house. An odd thing has been built in above your front entrance; it has always intrigued me."

I had no idea to what he was alluding and I was amazed that he apparently knew our house better than I did myself. The keystone of the arch had certainly a coat-of-arms on it but it had been worn smooth during the centuries and had often been painted over; as far as I knew it had nothing to do with ourselves and our family history.

"I don't know anything about it," I said shyly. "It's a bird or something of the sort; it must be quite ancient. The house is supposed to have belonged to a monastery in the old days."

"That might well be so," he said, nodding. "Have a good look at it. I think the bird is a sparrow-hawk."

We walked on; I felt very constrained. Suddenly Demian laughed as if something comic had occurred to him.

"Yes, I was there during your lesson," he burst out. "The story of Cain who bore the mark on his forehead, wasn't it? Do you like it?"

No; it was rare for me to like anything we had to learn. I did not however dare to confess it; for I felt I was being addressed by a grown-up. I said I liked the story quite well.

Demian slapped me on the back.

"You don't need to put on an act with me, dear chap. All the same the story is really very remarkable, much more so than most of the other stories that are taught in class. Your teacher did not say much about it – just the usual comment about God and sin and so on. But I believe . . ." he broke off and asked with a smile, "But are you interested?"

"Yes. I believe, then," he continued, "that this story of Cain can be interpreted differently. Most of the stories we are taught are valid and authentic but it is possible to see them from another angle than that of the teachers' and it gives them much more sense. You can't feel satisfied with this Cain for example and with the mark on his forehead as they explain it to us. Don't you agree? Someone may certainly kill his own brother in a quarrel, and he may panic afterwards and eat humble pie. But that he should be marked with a special 'sign' for his cowardice that acts as a kind of protection and inspires fear in everybody else is strange indeed."

"It is," I said, becoming interested in the subject. "But what other interpretation could one give the story?"

He struck me on the shoulder again.

"Quite simple. What happened and lay behind the whole origin of the story was the 'sign'. Here was a man who had something in his face that frightened other people. They did not dare lay hands on him; he impressed them, he and his children. It is virtually certain that he bore no actual mark on his brow like a post mark! Real life isn't as crude as that. Rather there was some hardly perceptible mark, a little more intelligence and self-possession in his eyes than people were accustomed to. This man had power and they all went in awe of him; he had a 'sign'. You can explain that how you will. People always want whatever is comfortable and puts them in the right. They were afraid of Cain's children; they bore a sign. So the sign was not interpreted for what it really was but the contrary. They said that people with this sign were odd, as indeed they were. Men of courage and character always seem very sinister to the rest. It was a sinister thing that a breed of strange, fearless people should be going about, and so they attached a nickname and a myth to this family as a way of taking revenge and ridding themselves of guilt for all the fear they had experienced. Do you see?"

"Yes – that means then that Cain was not really evil? And the whole Bible story isn't really authentic?"

"Yes and no. These ancient stories are always true in a sense, but they are not always properly recorded or given a correct interpretation. In short, I consider Cain to be a fine fellow and they pinned this story on to him merely because they were afraid of him. The story had its basis in hearsay, the kind of thing people bandy about, and it was true in so far as Cain and his children really bore some kind of mark and were different from other people."

I was astounded.

"And do you believe that the business of the slaying isn't true either?" I asked, fascinated.

"Oh yes, that's certainly true. The strong man slew the weak. But we may well doubt whether it was his brother. It isn't important. Ultimately all men are brothers. Thus a strong man slew a weak man. Perhaps it was the deed of a hero, perhaps not. At all events the other weaklings were now filled with fear, complained bitterly and when they were asked, 'Why do you not slay him too?' they did not reply, 'Because we are cowards,' but, 'We cannot. He has a sign. God hath branded him!' The fraud must have originated somehow like that ... But, I'm keeping you. Goodbye then!"

He turned into the Altgasse and left me standing there more baffled than I had ever been before in my life. Almost as soon as he had gone everything he had said seemed utterly incredible. Cain a noble man, Abel a coward! The brand of Cain, a mark of distinction! It was absurd; it was blasphemous and wicked. Where had God been? Had He not accepted Abel's sacrifice, did He not love Abel? No, it was all nonsense. Demian had wanted to fool me, lead me on and get me into trouble. He was a devilish clever fellow and could talk, but he couldn't put that one over.

I have never before given so much thought to a Bible story or any other for that matter. It was a long time since I had forgotten Franz Kromer so completely, for hours, for a whole evening in fact. At home I read the story once again as it was written in the Bible; it was short and unambiguous, and it was quite mad to look for any special, hidden meaning. At that rate, any murderer could masquerade as a favoured one of God! No, it was nonsense. It was just Demian's easy and attractive way of telling these things as if everything were self-evident; and then that look in his eyes!

There was something very wrong with me. I had lived in a wholesome and unsullied world; I had been a kind of Abel and now I was stuck so deeply in the 'other' world, I had fallen and sunk and yet, at heart, I could not really help it. How was this? And now a memory flashed through my mind which left me almost breathless. On that fatal evening when my present trouble had begun and I had been with my father, I had suddenly seen through his world of light and wisdom! Indeed I myself who was Cain and bore that sign had imagined that the sign was nothing to be ashamed of but a distinction rather and that because of my wickedness and misfortune I stood higher than my father, higher than the pious and righteous.

I did not think the matter out as definitely as that, but my thought was composed of all these elements; it was a stirring of strange emotions that hurt me and filled me with pride at the same time.

When I considered how strangely Demian had spoken of the fearless and the cowards, how oddly he had interpreted the sign on Cain's brow, how his remarkable adult eyes had lit up, the question flashed through my mind whether this Demian himself was not a kind of Cain? Why did he defend him if he didn't share the same feelings? Why had he this power in his eyes? Why did he speak so scornfully of the 'others,' the timid souls who after all were the pious and chosen ones of the Lord?

These thoughts went round and round in my head. It was a stone dropped into a well, and the well was my youthful soul. And for a long time this matter of Cain, the murder and the 'sign' formed an outlet for my attempts at recognition, my doubts and criticism.

I observed that Demian exercised a fascination over the other boys too. I had not breathed a word to anyone about the Cain business but the rest also seemed to be interested in him. At all events there were many rumours in circulation about the 'new' boy. If I only knew them all, I thought, each one would throw some light on his character and have some significance. But I merely knew that Demian's mother was reported to be very wealthy. It was also said that neither she nor her son ever attended church. One boy wondered whether they might not be Jews but they could equally well be Mohammedans. Tales were also current of Max Demian's physical prowess. He certainly had greatly humiliated the strongest boy in his class who had challenged him to a fight and called him a coward when he refused to fight. Those who were present said Demian had just taken him by the scruff of the neck with one hand and squeezed hard, whereupon the boy had gone white and crept off. He was unable to use his arm for days afterwards. The whole of one evening it was rumoured that he had died. For a time no assertion was too extravagant to be believed, everything about him was amazing and exciting. Then they had enough, temporarily at any rate. Not much later there was further gossip among us; some boys reported that Demian associated with girls and 'knew everything.'

Meanwhile my business with Franz Kromer followed its inevitable course. I could not escape him, for even when he left me in peace for a few days I was still bound to him. He haunted my dreams like my own shadow and any spell that he failed to cast over me in reality my imagination allowed him to cast in those dreams in which I became utterly his slave. I lived in them – I was always a great dreamer – and I used up my health and strength more in these shadows than in real life. A recurrent nightmare was that Kromer was torturing me, spitting and kneeling on me and, what was worse, leading me on to serious crimes – or rather not so much leading me on as compelling me by sheer force of personality. The most horrible feature of these nightmares from which I would awake, half-crazy, was a murderous attack on my father. Kromer sharpened a knife and put it in my hand and we stood behind the trees of an avenue lying in wait for someone. But when that person approached and Kromer conveyed to me by pinching my arm that this was the man I had to stab, I saw that it was my father. Then I would wake up.

Although preoccupied with these things, I certainly did still think about Cain and Abel but I gave little thought to Demian. When he first approached me, it was, oddly enough, likewise in a dream. Once again I was dreaming of torture and violence of which I was the victim, but this time it was Demian who knelt on me. And – this was a new feature and deeply impressed me – everything that I had resisted and that had caused me pain when Kromer was my tormentor I suffered gladly at Demian's hands with a feeling compounded as much of ecstasy as of fear. I dreamed it twice but the third time I found Franz back in his accustomed role.

I have long been unable to separate what I experienced in these dreams from the reality. Be that as it may, my bad relations with Kromer followed their course and were not at an end when I had paid off the sum owing to him with the fruits of my petty thefts. No; he now knew about these thefts for he pestered me with questions about the source of the money, and I was more in his hands than ever. He frequently threatened to tell my father everything but even then my fear was hardly as great as my profound regret that I had not told father myself at the beginning. Meantime, miserable though I was, I did not regret it all, at least not the whole time, and sometimes I believed that it was fated to happen in this way. My destiny hung over me and it was useless for me to try to escape.

Presumably my parents were considerably distressed while this situation continued. A strange spirit had come over me; I no longer fitted into our community with which I had previously been so closely bound up and I was often overcome with a wild hankering for it as for some kind of lost paradise. My mother, it was true, treated me more like a wayward than a sick child, but I was better able to judge from my sisters' attitude how matters really stood. This attitude of extreme indulgence towards me caused me infinite distress because it made it plain to me that I was considered as one in some way 'possessed,' more to be pitied than blamed for his condition but one, nevertheless, in whom the Devil had taken up his quarters. I felt that they were praying for me more than ever before and I was conscious of the futility of their prayers. I often felt a burning need for relief, a longing for sincere confession, but I knew in advance that I would be unable to tell and explain it properly either to my mother or father. I knew that it would all be accepted sympathetically, that they would be sorry for me but would not understand and that the whole thing would be regarded as an aberration, whereas in truth it was fate.

I realize that many people will be unable to credit a child not yet eleven years old with such feelings, but this story is not intended for them. I am recounting it to those who have a better understanding of human nature. The grown-up who has learnt to translate a part of his feelings into thoughts, misses these thoughts in the child and therefore finally denies even the experiences themselves. But I have rarely felt and suffered more deeply than at that time.

One rainy day I had been ordered by my tormentor to go to the town square. There I stood and waited, shuffling my feet among the wet chestnut leaves that were still falling from the wet trees. I had not any money but had put two pieces of cake to one side to take along so that at any rate I might be able to give Kromer something. I was used to standing in a corner and waiting for him, often for a very long time, and I put up with it the way one learns to tolerate the inevitable.

At length Kromer came up to me. He did not stay long. He dug me in the ribs a few times, laughed, took the cake, even offered me a damp cigarette and was more friendly than usual.

"Ah, yes," he said as he was leaving me, "before I forget, you might bring your sister along next time, your elder sister I mean. What is her name by the way?"

I failed to grasp his point and made no reply. I looked at him surprised.

"Don't you get me? You are to bring your sister."

"Yes, Kromer, but it's no good. I won't be allowed to do so and she wouldn't come in any case."

His proposal did not surprise me; I saw it for what it

was, a ruse and a pretext. It was the sort of thing he was always doing – demanding the impossible, frightening and humiliating me and then gradually relenting. I had to buy myself off with money or some gift.

This time however he was quite different. He was scarcely angry at all over my refusal.

"Well," he remarked perfunctorily, "think it over. I would like to meet your sister. All you need to do is to bring her out for a walk and then I will come up to you. I'll whistle for you tomorrow and then we can discuss it again."

When he had gone something of the nature of his request suddenly dawned on me. I was still completely a child in these matters but I knew from hearsay that boys and girls when they were a little older could do certain secret and improper things together. It flashed on me all at once how monstrous it was. My resolution never to be party to such a thing was made on the spot. But what would happen and how Kromer would take his revenge on me I did not dare to think. It was the beginning of a new martyrdom for me, there were still worse things in store.

Inconsolable, I walked across the empty square with my hands in my pockets. Further torments and slavery.

I had reached that point in my thoughts when a deep, cheerful voice hailed me. I was startled and began to run. Some one was pursuing me; a hand fell gently on my shoulder from behind. It was Max Demian.

I capitulated.

"Oh! It's you!" I said doubtfully. "You gave me such a fright!"

He looked at me. Never had his expression seemed more like that of a grown-up, a superior and perspicacious being than at that moment. We had not spoken to each other for a long time.

"I'm sorry," he said in his polite yet firm way, "but look here, you oughtn't to let yourself be frightened like that."

"But you can't always help it."

"So it seems. But see here; when you shrink back from someone who hasn't done you any harm, then that someone begins to think. He is surprised; it makes him inquisitive. The someone thinks that you are remarkably nervous and comes to the conclusion that people are always like that when they are afraid. Cowards are always afraid, but I don't believe that you're a coward, are you? Certainly you aren't a hero either. There are some things that you are afraid of; there are people too of whom you are afraid. And you oughtn't to be. No; one should never be afraid of any man. You're not afraid of me? Or are you?"

"Oh no, not at all."

"There you are. But there *are* people you are frightened of?"

"I don't know ... leave me alone, what do you want of me?"

I quickened my pace with thoughts of flight but he kept up with me and I felt him glancing at me out of the corner of his eye.

"Let us assume," he began again, "that I am well-disposed towards you. At any rate you've no need to be afraid of me. Right then. I'd like to carry out an experiment with you, it is quite a light-hearted one and you may learn something that will prove very useful. Listen then! I often try out an art which is known as thought-reading. There's no black magic about it but if you don't know how it is done it seems uncanny. You can cause people considerable surprise too. Well, we will try the experiment. Now, I am fond of you or interested in you and I would like to discover what it's like inside you. To do this I have already taken the initial step. I frightened you. You are therefore in a nervous state. How has that come about? You don't need to be afraid of anybody. When you are afraid of someone it means you have provided that someone with some kind of lever. You have done something wrong for example and the other person knows this and by this means has acquired a hold over you. You understand? It's clear enough, isn't it?"

I looked up helplessly at his face which was as serious and intelligent as ever and good-natured too, but there was no tenderness in his manner which was severe. It had an element of righteousness or something akin to it. I was hardly aware of what was happening to me. He stood over me like a magician.

"Have you got my meaning?" he asked again.

I nodded. I was unable to speak.

"I told you thought-reading seems comic but it comes about quite naturally. I could for example tell you pretty accurately what you thought about me when I once told you the story of Cain and Abel. But that has nothing to do with the present case. I also consider it possible that you once dreamed about me. But let's forget that too. You're a bright lad and most of them are so stupid! I enjoy an occasional chat with an intelligent person in whom I can have confidence. Do you mind?"

"Of course not. But I don't understand."

"Let's keep to our light-hearted experiment. So, we have discovered this much. The boy, X, is frightened – he is afraid of someone – he probably shares a secret with this other fellow which is very uncomfortable for him. Isn't that, roughly speaking, the situation?"

I succumbed to his voice and influence as in a dream. All I could do was to nod. It was like a voice which could only emanate from myself. A voice, indeed, that knew everything better and more clearly than myself.

Demian slapped me on the back.

"So that's what it is? I thought it might be. Now, just one question. Can you tell me the name of the boy who went off a few moments ago?"

I was terrified, my threatened secret curled back inside me, afraid to come out into the daylight.

"What kind of boy? There wasn't any boy there – only me."

He laughed.

"Tell me!" he laughed. "What's his name?"

"Do you mean Franz Kromer?" I whispered.

He gave a satisfied nod.

"Good! You're a sensible chap. We'll become friends yet. But first I must tell you something. This Kromer or whatever his name is, is a rotter. I can tell by his face that he's a scoundrel! What do you think?"

"Oh yes," I sighed, "he's a bad lot all right, he's the Devil himself! But he mustn't hear about this. For God's sake he mustn't hear. Do you know him? Does he know you?"

"Don't worry! He's gone off and he doesn't know me – not yet. But I'd like to make his acquaintance. Does he go to the village school?"

"Yes."

"What class?"

"The top class. But don't say anything to him! Please, please, don't say anything!"

"Don't worry, nothing will happen to you. I don't suppose you would care to tell me a bit more about this Kromer fellow?"

"I can't! No, leave me!"

He was silent for a while.

"It's a pity," he said. "We could have carried the experiment one stage further. But I won't torment you. But you do realize, don't you, that your fear of him is all wrong? A fear of that kind can be our ruin, we've got to get rid of it, *you've* got to get rid of it and you *must* get rid of it if you're going to be any good. Do you understand?"

"Certainly, you are quite right . . . but it's no good. You don't know . . ."

"But you've seen that I know a good deal more than you thought. Do you owe him some money?"

"Yes, that as well, but that's not the main thing. I can't tell you, I can't."

"Wouldn't it help then if I gave you the sum of money which you owe him? I could easily do so."

"No, it's not that. And I implore you not to say anything about it to anyone. Not a word! You're making me very unhappy."

"You can rely on me, Sinclair. You can tell me your secret some other time."

"Never, never," I cried loudly.

"Just as you like. All I mean is that perhaps you may tell me more about it later. Voluntarily of course! You don't think I'd behave like Kromer, I hope?"

"Oh, no – but you know practically nothing about it!"

"Nothing at all. I am merely thinking about it. And, believe me, I would never follow Kromer's example. And you don't owe *me* anything."

We did not speak for a long time and I calmed down. But I found Demian's knowledge all the more puzzling.

"I'm going home now," he said, gathering his coat closer round him in the rain. "There's just one more thing that I would like to say, since we have got so far – you ought to get rid of the fellow! If there's nothing else for it, kill him! I should be pleased and impressed if you did. I would even lend you a hand."

My fear returned again. The story of Cain suddenly recurred to me. The whole thing seemed sinister to me, and I began to weep silently. Too many strange things were going on round me.

"Good then," laughed Max Demian. "Go home now! We'll do something, though murder would be the simplest. The simplest thing is always the best in such cases. You're in bad hands with friend Kromer."

I found my way home and felt as if I had been away for a year. Everything looked different. Between me and Kromer stood something like the future, something in the nature of hope. I was no longer alone! And now for the first time I saw how terribly alone I had been with my secret all those weeks. And something occurred to me over which I had often pondered, that a confession to my parents would merely relieve me without entirely redeeming me. Now I had almost confessed to some one else, a stranger, and a feeling of relief rushed at me like a strong perfume.

For all that, my fear was still far from conquered and I was prepared for a long series of terrifying disputes with my enemy. That was why it seemed remarkable that matters were being allowed to drift so discreetly and undisturbed.

For a whole day, two, three days, a week there was no sound of Kromer's whistle in front of our house. I could not believe it and was continually on the watch in case he might suddenly reappear when he was least expected. But he continued to absent himself. Mistrustful of my new freedom, I could not really believe in it until at length I met Franz Kromer. He was coming towards me down the Seilergasse. When he saw me, his features were distorted in an ugly grimace, and without more ado, he turned round in order to avoid meeting me.

It was an astonishing moment for me. My enemy was running away from me! The Devil was afraid of me! I felt a thrill of joy and surprise.

Demian showed himself again during those days. He waited for me in front of the school.

"Hello," I said.

"Good morning, Sinclair. I only wanted to hear how you were getting on. Kromer is leaving you alone, isn't he?"

"Are *you* responsible for that? But how then? How? I can't understand it. He's kept right away."

"That's good. If he should turn up again – I don't

think he will, but he's an insolent fellow – just tell him not to forget Demian."

"But what's the connection? Did you pick a quarrel with him and thrash him?"

"No, I'm not keen on that sort of thing. I've merely been talking to him as I did to you and made it plain that it is to his own advantage to leave you alone."

"Oh, but you haven't paid him any money?"

"No, sonny. You had tried that method already."

He made off, though I badly wanted to question him and I was left with the oppressive feeling he always gave me; it was an odd mixture of gratitude and awe, admiration and fear, consent and inward hostility.

I resolved to see him again soon so that I could discuss it all with him as well as the Cain business. But this was not to be.

Gratitude is certainly not a virtue that I believe in and to expect it from a child would seem false. So the utter ingratitude I showed towards Max Demian does not surprise me. Today I have no doubt whatsoever that I should never have recovered, but would have been ruined for life if he had not freed me from Kromer's clutches. Even at that time I was conscious of this liberation as the greatest experience of my young life – but I deserted my liberator as soon as he had accomplished the miracle.

There was nothing remarkable, as I have just affirmed, about my ingratitude. The one strange thing was my lack of curiosity. How was it possible for me to live another day without drawing any closer to the secrets with which Demian had brought me into contact? How could I resist the curiosity to hear more about Cain, more about Kromer, more about thought-reading?

It is hardly comprehensible and yet it was so. I suddenly saw myself extricated from the snares of the Devil, and saw the world lying bright and joyful before me; I was no longer succumbing to attacks of fear and suffocating palpitations. The spell was broken; I was no longer damned and tormented, I was a schoolboy again. My nature was striving to regain its equilibrium and composure, seeking above all else to put away from me and forget whatever was ugly and threatening. The whole long story of my guilt and fright was slipping away from my memory with incredible rapidity without leaving behind any scars or ill effects.

I can also understand today why I was trying to forget my saviour and helper with equal rapidity. From the valley of sorrows of my damnation, from the frightful slavery with Kromer, I was fleeing back with every fibre of my damaged soul to where I had been happy and contented – the lost paradise that was now opening up again, the untroubled world of mother and father, to my sisters, the smell of cleanliness, the at-oneness with the God of Abel.

Already on the day following my short conversation with Demian when I was finally fully convinced of my newly won freedom and had no fear of losing it again, I did what I had so often and so desperately wanted – I confessed. I went to my mother, I showed her the money-box with its damaged lock and filled with counters instead of money and I told her how long I had bound myself through my own guilt to an evil tormentor. She did not wholly grasp my story but she saw the money-box, the change in my appearance, heard the change in my tone of voice and felt that I was cured and restored to her.

And now with heightened emotions I underwent the ceremony of my re-admittance to the fold, the Prodigal Son's home-coming. Mother took me along to father, the story was repeated, questions and exclamations of praise were showered on me; both parents patted me on the head and breathed great sighs of relief. Everything was marvellous, everything was like the fairy-tales, everything was restored to a wonderful harmony.

I escaped into this harmony with real emotion. I could never be thankful enough at having regained my peace of mind and my parents' confidence. I became a model home-boy, played more than ever with my sisters and at evening prayers I sang all the favourite hymns with the feelings of the home-comer who is saved. It came from the heart; there was nothing false about it.

And yet my house was not really in order. It was that fact alone that really accounted for my neglectful attitude towards Demian, for it was to *him* that I should have confessed. The confession would have been less exaggerated, less emotional but much more fruitful for me. As it was, I was clinging with all my roots to my former earthly paradise; I had returned home and had been accepted in grace. But it was not Demian's world nor was he suited to it. He too – though in a different way from Kromer – was a 'tempter' and moreover my link with the second, evil world with which I never wanted to have anything more to do. I could not and would not abandon Abel and glorify Cain now that I myself had once more become an Abel.

That was the outward connection. The inner, however, was that I had escaped from Kromer's and the Devil's hand but not through any power and effort of my own. I had tried to tread the paths of the world and they had been too slippery for me. Now, as the grip of a friendly hand had saved me, I retreated to my mother's lap and the security of a pious and hedged-in childhood, without so much as a glance at the world outside. I made myself into someone younger, more dependent and childish than I was. I had to replace my dependency on Kromer by a new one for I was unable to walk alone. In the blindness of my heart, I chose to be dependent on my father and mother, on all the familiar and much cherished 'world of light.' I already knew that it was not the only one. If I had not followed this course, I would have had to stick to Demian and confide in him. That I did not do so seemed to me at that time on account of my justifiable mistrust of his strange ideas, in reality it was entirely because of fear. For Demian would have been far more exacting than my parents; by means of persuasion, admonition, mockery and sarcasm he had done his best to foster an independent spirit in me. Alas, how well I realise that today. Nothing in the world is more distasteful to a man than to follow the path that leads to himself.

Yet six months later I was unable to resist the temptation, and during a walk I asked my father what one was to make of the fact that many people considered Cain better than Abel.

He was taken aback and explained that this was an interpretation which was by no means new to our time. It was one that had arisen already in Old Testament times and it had been taught among sects which included the 'Cainites.' But this heresy was, of course, merely an attempt on the part of the Devil to destroy our beliefs. For if one believed in the right of Cain and the wrong of Abel, then it followed that God had committed an error, that the God of the Bible was not the true and only God but a false God. In reality the Cainites were reputed to have taught and preached something of the sort but this false doctrine had long disappeared and he was surprised that a school-friend of mine should have heard anything about it. At all events he warned me gravely against harbouring such ideas.

There is much that I could say about the happy and tender incidents in my childhood days, the sense of security which I enjoyed with my parents, my childish affection and carefree, irresponsible existence in a gentle and affectionate ambience. But my interest is reserved for the steps that I took in my life towards self-realization. All the pleasant points of repose, islands of happiness, paradises whose magic was not unknown to me can remain, as far as I am concerned, in the enchanted distance; for it is not a world that I have any particular desire to re-enter.

While I linger here in my boyhood days I am speaking of things that were new experiences and carried me forward with them.

These impulses came without exception from the 'other' world, were always attended by fear, constraint and bad conscience; they were always revolutionary and constituted a threat to the peace of mind in which I would gladly have continued to live.

Then came years when once again I could no longer hide from myself the existence of the old urge driving me back into the world of light to hide there. My gradual awareness of sex loomed up before me, as it does before everyone, as an enemy and destroyer, as something forbidden, corrupt and sinful. What my curiosity had hoped for, what my dreams, desire and fear aroused in me, the great secret of puberty, did not fit into the circumscribed happiness of my childhood's joy.

I behaved like everybody else. I led the double life of the child who is no longer a child. My conscious self lived in the homely and sanctioned, my conscious self denied the new world that was darkling round me. Side by side with this, however, I lived in dreams, actions, desires of a subterranean kind over which my conscious life nervously constructed a series of bridges, for my childhood's world was falling apart. Like almost all parents, mine made no attempt to foster the stirring roots of life; no reference was made to them. All they did was to go to endless trouble to bolster my hopeless attempts to deny reality and continue to dwell in a child's world which was becoming more and more unreal and false. It may be that parents cannot do much about it, and I am not trying to reproach mine. It was my own affair to see myself through and find my own way and like most well-brought up children I managed it badly.

Every man goes through this period of crisis. For the average man it is the point in his life when the demands of his own fate are most at odds with his environment, when the way ahead is most hardly won. For many it is the only time in their lives when they experience the dying and resurrection which is our lot, during the decay and slow collapse of childhood when we are abandoned by everything we love, and suddenly feel the loneliness and deathly cold of the world around us. And a great many people stay for ever hanging on to this cliff and cling desperately their whole life through to the irrevocable past, the dream of the lost paradise which is the worst and most ruthless of all dreams.

If I turn back the pages of my story, the sensations which announced the end of my childhood are too insignificant to be mentioned. The important thing was that the 'dark world,' the 'other world' was there again. What had once been Franz Kromer was now embedded in me. And in this way the 'other world' was gaining power over me from outside.

Several years had gone by since the Kromer affair. At that time the dramatic and guilty period of my life lay far behind me and seemed to have melted away like a brief nightmare. Franz Kromer had long vanished out of my life; I hardly gave him a thought even when I met him. However, the other important figure in my tragic story, Max Demian, was no longer absent from my circle, although for a long time he stood at the perimeter, visible but out of effective range. Only gradually did he come closer and radiate his strength and influence.

I am trying to think what I remember of Demian at that time. It may be that for a year or more I did not once speak to him. I avoided him and on the few occasions when we did meet, he merely nodded to me. Sometimes I got the impression that there was a faint ring of derision and ironical reproach in this friendlienss but it may have been my fancy. The experience I had shared with him and the strange influence which he had exerted on me were as though forgotten by both of us.

I am trying to conjure up his figure and now when I think of him, I see that he was indeed present in my life. I can see him on his way to school, alone or among others of the senior boys, and I can see him strange, lonely and quiet, wandering aloof in their midst, surrounded by his own aura, a law unto himself. Nobody liked him, no one was on intimate terms with him except his mother and even with her his relations seemed to be those of an adult rather than a child. The teachers mostly left him to himself; he was a bright pupil but he made no attempt to please anybody, and now and again we heard of sayings, comments or retorts which he was rumoured to have made to one or other of the teachers which, as examples of forthrightness and irony, left little to be desired.

As I close my eyes and reflect, I see his image rise up before me. Where was it? Oh yes, I have it now. He was in the narrow lane in front of our house. One day I saw him standing there, notebook in hand, sketching. He was drawing the old coat-of-arms with the bird above our front entrance. And as I stood concealed behind the curtain, watching him, I felt a deep admiration for that keen, cool, bright face turned towards the coat-of-arms; it was the face of a full-grown man, a scholar or artist, deliberate and purposeful, strangely clear and self-possessed and with a discriminating eye.

I see him on another occasion a little later on, in the street, when we were on our way home from school and had stopped to look at a fallen horse. It lay still, harnessed to the shaft in front ot a peasant-cart, snorting plaintively in the air with dilated nostrils, bleeding from a hidden wound so that the white street-dust at its side was being slowly stained dark red. As I turned away with a feeling of nausea, I noticed Demian's expression. He had not thrust himself to the front but stood right at the back, looking elegant and at ease as usual. His glance seemed directed at the horse's head, and again it showed that deep, quiet, almost fanatical yet passionate absorption. I could not help staring at him for some moments and it was then that I felt aware of a very uncanny sensation in my remote consciousness. I saw Demian's face and remarked that it was not a boy's face but a man's and then I saw, or rather became aware, that it was not really the face of a man either; it had something different about it, almost a feminine element. And for the time being his face seemed neither masculine nor childish, neither old nor young but a hundred years old, almost timeles and bearing the mark of other periods of history than our own. Animals might look thus, trees or stars. I did not know then, of course, I did not feel exactly what I am writing about it now, as an adult, but it was something of the kind. Perhaps he was handsome, perhaps I found him attractive, perhaps he repelled me too, I could not even be sure of that. All I saw was that he was different from the rest of us, that he was like an animal, a spirit or an image. I cannot describe him except to say that he was different, unimaginably different from the rest of us. My memory is a blank about everything else and perhaps even what I have described is to some extent gleaned from later impressions.

Only when I was several years older did I come into close touch with him. Contrary to the usual custom, Demian had not been confirmed with other boys of his year, and once again rumours had been rife. It was said that he was a Jew or a heathen, more likely, and some boys were convinced that he and his mother had either no religion or belonged to a fanatic and disreputable sect. In this connexion I remembered having heard that he was suspected of being his mother's lover. Probably the fact of the matter was that he had been brought up without any particular religion and this caused everybody to forecast an unsavoury future for him. At all events his mother decided not to allow him to be confirmed until two years after the boys in his class. So it came about that for months he attended the same confirmation classes as I did.

For a time I completely avoided him; I did not want to have anything to do with him; too many rumours and secrets hung about him, and I was particularly disturbed by my feeling of indebtedness towards him ever since the Kromer affair. I had enough to do with my own secrets. The confirmation classes coincided with the critical period of my initiation into sex, and against my best intentions my interest in matters of piety was thereby considerably prejudiced. The things the pastor spoke about lay remote in a quiet, holy reality of their own; all very fine and precious, doubtless, but to me they lacked the reality and excitement that the other world possessed in the highest degree.

The more indifferent this attitude made me towards religious instruction, the more interested I became in Demian. A bond seemed to exist between us. And I must choose this moment to follow up that thread in my life as accurately as I can. As far as I remember, it all began one day in the early morning class when the light was still burning in the schoolroom. Our scripture teacher, a pastor, had embarked on the story of Cain and Abel. I was still sleepy and only listening with half an ear. All at once the pastor began to hold forth about the mark of Cain in loud and excited tones. At that moment I became aware of a stirring-up inside me, a kind of challenge, and, looking up, I saw Demian's face turning round towards me from the front desks with that clear, eloquent glance of his which might be expressing scorn or gravity, you could not be sure which. He merely looked at me for a moment, and suddenly I gave the pastor's words my fullest attention, listened to him speaking of Cain and his mark, and felt deep within me the knowledge that the thing was not as he was teaching it, but that there was an alternative interpetation and that criticism of his view was justifiable.

A fresh bond was forged between Demian and myself in that moment. And, strangely enough, hardly was I aware of this spiritual closeness between us when I saw it translated as if by magic into physical closeness. I had no idea whether he had managed to arrange it in that way or whether it was fate – I firmly believed in strokes of fate at that time – but a few days later Demian had suddenly changed his place in the scripture class and sat directly in front of me. I can recall how I enjoyed smelling the fresh, delicate perfume of soap from his neck in the midst of the miserable workhouse atmosphere of the over-crowded schoolroom! And again, some days later he had changed places again and was sitting next to me where he stayed all through winter and spring.

The morning lessons now were utterly transformed. They no longer made me sleepy and bored. I looked forward to them. We would often listen to the pastor with the greatest concentration and a glance from my neighbour sufficed to draw my attention to any remarkable story or strange saying. Another kind of glance, a very meaning one, sufficed to awaken critical doubts inside me.

All too often however we were inattentive pupils and paying little heed to the lesson. Demian was always a model of good behaviour in his relations both to masters and fellow-pupils. I never caught him indulging in the usual schoolboy pranks, never heard him guffaw or chatter or incur the teacher's displeasure. But quietly and more by means of signs and glances than whisperings he contrived to make me share in his preoccupations. Some of these were most odd.

He told me, for example, which of the other boys interested him and how he made them the objects of his study. He knew a number of them very well. Sometimes he would say to me before the lesson, "If I give you a signal with my thumb, so and so will turn round and look at us, or scratch his neck, and similar things." During the lesson, often when I had forgotten all about it, Max would suddenly jerk his thumb in an odd way for my benefit and I would steal a rapid glance at the boy he was indicating and on each occasion the boy would make the gesture willed upon him as if he were a puppet on strings. I plagued Max to try this trick on a master but he refused. Once however, when I came into the lesson and told him I had not learned my 'prep' and desperately hoped that the pastor would not ask me any questions, he came to my rescue. The pastor was looking for a pupil to recite a passage of the catechism, and his roving eye alighted on my guilty face. He slowly strode up to me, pointed his finger in my direction and already had my name on his lips when all at once he became distracted, looked uncomfortable and fingered his collar, walked up to Demian who resolutely met his glance, and seemed to want to ask him something. But he quietly turned away again, cleared his throat a few times and chose another pupil.

Only gradually did I become aware that at the same time as I was finding amusement in these jokes, I was myself a frequent victim of a similar trick. I would have the feeling on my way to school that Demian was walking a short distance behind me and when I turned round I discovered he was there in reality.

"Can you really make another person think what you want?" I asked him.

He answered quite readily in his quiet, factual, grown-up way.

"No." he said. "We haven't free will, whatever the pastor makes out. The other person can't think what he will any more than I can make him think what *I* will. It is possible however to think hard about someone and frequently guess what he is thinking and feeling and then, more often than not, one can anticipate his next move. It is simple enough only people don't know it. Naturally you need practice. There is, for example, a species of moth in which the females are much less common than the males. Moths breed like all animals, the male fertilizes the female who lays the eggs. If you get hold of a female of this particular species of moth – the experiment has often been tried by naturalists – the males come flying to this female in the night for hours on end. Just think! For several miles around these males smell the only female in the district. We try to find an explanation but it is difficult. They must have a sense of smell or something; it is like the way good gun dogs can pick up and follow what would appear to be an imperceptible scent. Do you get the idea? It's the kind of inexplicable thing that nature abounds in. This, however, I can say: if the females were as common as the males among these moths, the latter would not have such a fine nose! They've acquired that merely because they've trained themselves to it. If an animal or a man bends his whole will to a certain end, he achieves it. It's as simple as that. And that is how it is in the present case. Examine a man closely enough and you'll soon know more about him than he does himself."

It was on the tip of my tongue to mention the word

'thought-reading' and remind him of the scene with Kromer which was now so remote; but the subject had become taboo between us and neither he nor I ever made the vaguest allusion to the fact that several years ago he had seriously concerned himself with my life. It was as if no previous relationship had ever existed between us, as if each of us presumed the other had forgotten about it. Indeed it happened on one or two occasions that as we were walking along the street we encountered Franz Kromer yet we neither of us exchanged a glance nor mentioned a word about him.

"But what is this 'will' business?" I asked him. "You say that we don't possess free will but then again you say one only needs to fix one's will resolutely on some objective to achieve it. It doesn't make sense. If I am not master of my own will, then I am not in a position to direct it here or there as I wish."

He slapped me on the back, as he always did when he was pleased with me.

"Good for you; I'm glad you asked!" he said laughing. "You must always ask; you must always doubt. But it is a very simple matter. If, for example, a night-moth wanted to direct his will on a star or some equally remote object, he would fail. He doesn't even make the attempt. He confines his search to what makes sense for him, that is, what he needs, what is indispensable to him. And he achieves the miraculous – he develops a magic sixth sense which no other creature possesses but him! There is more scope and interest in the case of human beings than of animals. But even we are bounded within a pretty narrow circle beyond which we may not stray. It is all very well for me to imagine this or that, imagine I will get to the north pole or some such idea but I can focus my will strongly enough on it only if the wish is really so deeply rooted within me that it permeates my whole being. Once that is the case, once you feel what is required of you from within, all is well and you can harness your will like an obedient horse. It is no use, for example, my undertaking to 'will' that our pastor shall take to wearing spectacles. It would be reducing the thing to a game. But when that time in autumn I made the firm resolution to be shifted from my desk in the front of the class, it was effective. A boy suddenly turned up whose name preceded mine in the alphabet and who had been away ill before, and as someone had to take his place, I was given it because my will was ready to seize the opportunity."

"Yes," I said, " I remember having a special feeling at the time. From the moment when we took an interest in each other, you began to get closer to me, literally. But how did it come about? You did not come and sit by me straight away; you were content to sit on the bench in front of me occasionally, weren't you? Why was that?"

"Yes; that is so; I did not know myself where I wanted to be when I wanted to shift from my original place. I merely knew that I wanted to sit further back. It was my wish to get closer to you and that, to begin with, was quite unconscious. At the same time your will accorded with mine and helped me. Only when I found myself sitting in front of you did I realize that my wish was only half fulfilled and that my sole wish had been to sit next to you."

"But there wasn't a new boy joining the class just then."

"No, but I was merely doing what I wanted at that time and sat down next to you without further thought. The boy with whom I changed places was too taken aback to object. And the pastor too noticed on one occasion that there had been a swop round – but every time he had to do with me something appeared to disturb him. He knew my name was Demian and that something was wrong and that since my name began with a 'D' I ought not to be sitting directly behind an 'S'! But the thought did not penetrate his consciousness because my will opposed it and because I continued to thwart him. He kept noticing that something was odd and the good man looked at me and tried to puzzle it out. But I had a simple expedient. I stared him out on each occasion. It's a treatment very few people can stand. They all become uncomfortable. If you want to get something out of someone and you look him in the eye, unexpectedly and resolutely and he doesn't become ill at ease, give it up! You'll never get anywhere with him, never. But that is a rare occurrence. In actual fact, I know only one person with whom it is ineffective."

"And who is that?" I asked him quickly.

He looked at me, his eyes narrowing as they did when he became thoughtful. Then he turned away and gave no reply, and though I was profoundly curious, I could not repeat the question.

I believe, however, that he had his mother in mind – he seemed very closely bound up with her. Yet he never as much as mentioned her name and never took me along to their house. I hardly knew what his mother looked like.

Many a time I attempted to imitate him and fix my will on something with such concentration that I was certain to achieve it. They were wishes which seemed urgent enough to me. But nothing happened; it didn't work. I could not bring myself to mention the matter to Demian. I should have found it impossible to confess my wishes to him. Nor did he ask me.

Meantime cracks had begun to appear in my religious faith. And yet my way of thought, which was very much dominated by Demian's influence, was very different from that of my fellow pupils who boasted a complete unbelief. For there were some such boys among us. They would say, for example, that it was ridiculous and unworthy of men to believe in a God and that stories like that of the Trinity and the Virgin birth were absurdities and that it was a scandal that such stuff was being hawked around in our times. But I did not share these views. Even where my doubts lay, I knew enough from my childhood's experience about the reality of a pious life such as my parents led and that it was neither unworthy nor hypocritical. Furthermore I felt then, as ever, the deepest awe before the truly religious. But Demian had accustomed me to considering and explaining the stories and articles of faith to myself in a less hide-bound and more personal and imaginative way; at any rate I gladly and willingly accepted the interpretations he urged on me. A good deal of it – such as the Cain episode – was indeed more than I could take, and on one occasion during the confirmation classes, he frightened me with an idea which was, if possible, even more startling. The teacher had been speaking of Golgotha. The Bible account of the passion and death of the Saviour had made a deep impression on me from my earliest days. Very often as a small boy round about the time of Good Friday, after my father had read the story of the passion to us, deeply moved and caught up, I had myself inhabited this sorrowful yet beautiful, pale, ghostly monstrously living world of Gethesemane and Mount Golgotha, and when I heard Bach's Matthew Passion, the mournful glowing power of the suffering of that hidden world had sent mystic shudders through me. Even today I find in this music and in the 'Actus tragicus' the epitome of all poetry and artistic expression.

At the end of the lesson in question Demian said to me thoughtfully, "This story has something about it that I don't like, Sinclair. Read it through, pass your tongue over it; there's an insipid element in it. It's this business of the two thieves. Wonderful how the three crosses stand next to each other on the Mount! But then why this tract-like story about the honest thief! First he was a criminal and had committed evil deeds, God knows what, and now he melts and takes part in tearful scenes of sorrow and repentance! What sense is there, I ask you, in such repentance when he is only two steps away from the grave? It's nothing but one of your pious moral tales, sugary and unconvincing, helped down with the grease of sentimentality and an edifying background. If you had to choose one of the two thieves today for a friend or consider which of the two you would prefer to trust, it certainly wouldn't be the snivelling convert. No, the other is the man and has real character. He despises a conversion which for a man in his position can only be a pretty speech, and pursues his own way to the end; he does not forswear the Devil who must have aided and abetted him at the eleventh hour. He has character and there are only too few people of character in the Bible. Perhaps he was a descendant of Cain's. Don't you agree?"

I was dumbfounded. I thought I was thoroughly familiar with the accepted story of the crucifixion and I now saw for the first time how little personal imagination I had brought to my hearing and reading of it. Yet Demian's new conception of it had for me a fatal ring; it threatened to overthrow the solid beliefs in me to which I felt I must cling. No; one could not turn everything upside down in that way, least of all the holy of holies. As usual, Demian noticed my opposition at once, but before I could say anything, he interrupted in a resigned voice, "I know, it's the old story, as long as you don't take the thing seriously! But there's something I would like to tell you: we are here dealing with one of the places where one is very conscious of the weakness of this religion. The point is that this God of both the Old and New Testaments is a wonderful figure but not what he purports to represent. He is all that is good, noble, he is the fatherly, the beautiful, the most high, the sentimental – all right! But the world consists also of other things which are merely ascribed to the Devil. And that half-section of the world is suppressed; it is never mentioned. It is the same as the way they celebrate God as the father of all life but the whole of sex-life which is the basis of life itself they are silent about, or indeed, whenever possible describe it as sinful and the work of the Devil! I have no objection to people honouring this God Jehovah, far from it. But I consider that we should sanctify and honour everything, the whole world, not merely this artificially separated, official half! Therefore alongside the divine service should be a Devil's service; that in my view would be right and proper. Otherwise you must create a God for yourself who embraces the Devil in himself and before whom you don't have to drop your eyes in shame when the most natural things in the world take place."

Contrary to his normal way, he had become almost violent but immediately afterwards, he smiled again and did not worry me further.

His words, however, went straight to my adolescent heart. What Demian had said about God and the Devil, about the godly-official and the suppressed Devil's world fitted in with my own ideas on the subject, my own myth, the conception I had of two worlds or two different halves of the world – the light and the dark. The realization that my problem was a problem of all humanity, a problem of all life and philosophy suddenly swept over me like a holy shadow and I was overcome with fear and awe when I saw how deeply my own personal life was caught up in the eternal stream of great ideas. This realization was not a joyful one although to some extent gratifying and corroborative. I found it hard and unpalatable because it contained a note of responsibility, of self-reliance, something beyond childish ideas; it implied standing alone.

For the first time in my life this deep secret was revealed to me and I told my friend about my idea of two 'different worlds' which I had held since childhood.

He saw immediately that I was entirely in sympathy with him and believed him to be right. But it was not his way to exploit this knowledge. He listened to me more attentively than he had ever done before and looked into my eyes until I had to avert mine. For in his gaze I saw once again the strange look, the animal-like timelessness that had no age.

"We'll talk about it another time," he said, forbearingly, "I see that you have thoughts you are unable to express. If that is so you must know that you too have not lived so far according to your own conception of life, and that is not a good thing. Only the ideas that we really *live* have any value. You have known that your 'permitted' world was only half of the world and you have tried to subjugate the second half after the manner of the priests and teachers. It will not be to your benefit! It benefits no one once he has begun to think."

I was profoundly moved.

"But," I almost shouted, "there are genuinely foul and forbidden things; you can't deny that! They are forbidden and we must renounce them. I know that there is murder and all manner of vice; but merely because it exists am I to go and become a criminal?"

"We won't continue this discussion today," said Demian, trying to appease. "Thou shalt certainly not kill – nor rape and kill girls. But you haven't yet reached the stage where you can understand what 'permitted' and 'forbidden' really means. You have only tracked down part of the truth. The rest is still to come, you can be quite sure of that. You have now had an urge in you for about a year that is stronger than anything else and is considered 'forbidden.' The Greeks and many other races on the other hand elevated this impulse into a godhead and honoured it at their great religious festivals. What is 'forbidden' is not permanently so; it can change. Even today any man can sleep with a woman once he has been to the priest with her and got married. With other races it is different, even nowadays. Therefore each one of us must discover for himself what is permitted and what is forbidden as far as he *himself* is concerned. It is possible never to do a 'forbidden' thing and yet be a real villain. And conversely.

Fundamentally it is merely a question of complacency! Whoever is too complacent to think for himself and be his own judge manages to accommodate himself to the 'shalt nots' as they exist at the present time. It is easy for him. But there are others who are conscious of the commandments in themselves; things are forbidden to them which every man does every day of his life, and other things are permitted to them which are otherwise prohibited. Every man must stand alone."

Demian suddenly seemed to regret having said so much, and he fell silent. I could already grasp to some extent, intuitively, what his reactions were. Although he was in the habit of expressing his ideas in an agreeable and apparently perfunctory manner, he could not tolerate 'talking for the sake of talking,' as he once told me. He was aware of my genuine interest but he felt that I treated clever conversation too much as a kind of game, in short, without due seriousness.

As I read the last word 'seriousness' which I have just written, another scene, the most striking I had ever experienced with Max Demian in those still half-childish days, leaps back to my mind.

The day of our confirmation approached, and the last lessons of the preparation by the pastor had to do with the Last Supper. It was a matter of great importance to the pastor who went to considerable pains to explain it; something of a sanctified mood certainly pervaded the atmosphere during those lessons. But it was precisely during those last periods of preparation that my thoughts were tied up elsewhere and, moreover, with the person of my friend. While I looked forward to the confirmation which was described to us as our solemn acceptance into the community of the Church, the thought rose urgently within me that the value of the last six months of religious preparation did not rest in what we had learned but in

Demian's proximity and influence. It was not into the Church that I was ready to be received but into something of an entirely different nature, an order of thought and personality which I felt must exist somewhere on earth and whose representative or apostle was Demian, my friend.

I endeavoured to suppress this thought; I was anxious to submit to the solemn ceremonial of the confirmation service with a certain dignity, whatever happened, and this did not seem to fit in at all with my new idea. Yet, do what I would, the thought was present and it gradually became linked in my mind with the approaching church ceremony. I was ready to comprehend it differently from the others; for me it was to signify my acceptance into a world of thought as I had learned to experience it in Demian.

It was in those days that I once more engaged in a vigorous argument with him; it was just before an instruction class. Demian was reserved by nature and found no pleasure in my talk which must have been both pompous and precocious.

"We talk too much," he said with unwonted seriousness. "Clever talk is of no value whatsoever. One merely gets further and further away from oneself and that is a crime. One should be able to crawl right into oneself like a tortoise."

Immediately afterwards we entered the schoolroom. The lesson began; I was careful to attend, and Demian did not try to distract me. After a while I began to be conscious of an odd feeling from the side where he sat next to me, a chill or void almost as if the place had somehow become unexpectedly empty. The feeling became oppressive and I turned round. My friend sat there upright with his shoulders braced back as usual. But he looked different and a kind of aura that was unfamiliar to me surrounded him. At first I thought his eyes were closed but I saw that in fact they were open. But they were not focused on anything; it was an unseeing gaze, dead and turned inwards or staring into the far distance. There he sat completely motionless; he did not even seem to be breathing; his lips might have been carved out of wood or stone. His face was pale, uniformly pale like stone and his brown hair was the most living thing about him. His hands lay on the desk in front of him, lifeless and still, like objects – pieces of stone or fruit, pale and motionless yet not limp; they were like good, firm pods that had formed round a robust, hidden life.

A shudder ran through me. He is dead, I thought. I almost said it aloud. But I knew that this was not so. My eyes were fixed on that pale, stone mask, spellbound, and I felt that here was the real Demian! What he had been before when he had gone around and chatted with me was only half of him, a person who for a time was playing a part, adapting himself to it, joining in the game to oblige me. The real Demian, however, looked like this – stone, age-old, animal-like, stone-like, handsome, cold, dead and yet with an alarming secret life within. And round him hung this aura of quiet emptiness, this ether and celestial space, this lonely death!

Now he has retreated completely within, I thought with a shudder. Never had I felt so lonely. I had no part in him; he was beyond my reach, farther away from me than if he had been on the remotest island in the world.

I could hardly grasp the fact that I was the only one who noticed it; I felt that they must all be looking, all shuddering! But no one paid any attention to him. He sat there like a graven image, as stiff as an idol and I cannot forget how when a fly alighted on his forehead and crawled over his nose and lips not a muscle of his face twitched.

Where had he withdrawn? What was he thinking; what was he feeling? Was he in heaven or in hell? It was an impossible question. When I saw him breathing and alive again at the end of the lesson and his glance met mine, he looked no different from before. Where had he returned from, where had he been? He appeared tired. The colour had come back to his face; his hands moved again but his brown hair looked somehow dull and lifeless.

The following days I gave myself up to a new exercise in my bedroom. I sat rigid on a chair and stared into space, held myself completely motionless and waited to see how long I could hold out and what I should experience. But I only succeeded in becoming tired and my eyelids began to prick.

Shortly afterwards came the confirmation service of which I can recollect nothing of importance.

Everything was transformed. My childhood tumbled about me in ruins. My parents regarded me with a certain embarrassment. My sisters had become almost strangers. A sense of disillusionment vitiated and blunted my normal feelings and pleasures, the garden had lost its fragrance, the forest its magic, the world stood round me like a clearance sale of old rubbish, insipid and with all its charm gone; books were so much paper, music was a noise. That is the way the leaves fall round an autumn tree; it is unaware of it, rain runs down it, it is subjected to sun or frost and life slowly retreats. It does not die. It waits.

It had been decided that I should go to another school after the holidays and leave home for the first time. Sometimes my mother approached me with particular tenderness, taking leave of me, as it were in advance, trying to inspire my heart with feelings of love and nostalgic memory. Demian had gone away. I was left alone.

IV Beatrice

Without having seen my friend again, I went to St. ——
after my holidays were over. My parents accompanied me
and with every possible solicitude for my welfare entrusted
me to the care of a master at the grammar school who was
in charge of a boarding-house. They would have been
frozen with horror if they had realized into what sort of
world they were introducing me.

The question as ever was whether, given time, a God-
fearing son and useful citizen could be made out of me or
whether my temperament would lead me astray. My last
attempt to be happy in the shadow of my father's house
and ambience had lasted quite a long time and at intervals
had been almost successful, but finally it failed utterly.

The unaccountable emptiness and abandonment which I
began to feel during the holidays after my confirmation –
and how familiar I was to become with that thin, desolate
atmosphere later! – was slow to leave me. My departure
from home was not too much of an ordeal; I felt ashamed
that I did not feel more homesick. My sisters wept for no
reason but I could not weep. I was surprised at myself.
I had always been a sensitive and essentially good child.
Now I had completely changed. I had acquired an attitude
of indifference towards the outside world and for days on
end I was preoccupied with inner voices and the dark,
forbidden streams which ran below the surface. I had
grown up very rapidly in the previous six months and now
gazed on to the world, lean, overgrown and unprepared.
My boyish charm had vanished, I even felt that it was
impossible for anyone to love me and I was out of love
with myself. I often felt a great longing for Demian; but
no less often I hated him, holding him responsible for the

impoverishment of my life which I was dragging round with me like a foul disease.

At first I was neither liked nor respected in our boarding-house. I was ragged to begin with, then avoided and regarded as a hypocrite and a disagreeable odd man out. I fell in with the part and even exaggerated it and grumbled myself into a kind of with-drawnness which the outsider must have taken for masculine cynicism, whereas, if the truth were told, I often succumbed to fits of gnawing melancholy and despair. In school I had to subsist on scraps of knowledge that had accumulated in my days at home since the class was somewhat less advanced than my previous one and I got used to regarding my fellow-pupils rather contemptuously as children.

It went on like this for a whole year and more; even the first holiday periods at home did not strike any new note and I was quite relieved to return to school again.

It was the beginning of November. During the weather typical of that season I had formed the habit of going on meditative walks on which I often enjoyed a kind of ecstasy, tinged with gloom, cynicism and self-depreciation. One evening in the damp, foggy twilight, I strode off through the environs of the town; the wide avenue in a public park stood completely deserted and seemed to beckon me to enter. The path lay thick with fallen leaves which smelt damp and acrid as I shuffled my feet among them with a kind of melancholy delight, and the distant trees loomed huge, shadowy and ghostlike out of the mist.

I stood irresolutely at the end of the avenue, stared eagerly into the dark foliage and the humid fragrance of death and decay which awoke and as it were answered some echo within me. How insipid life tasted!

A man joined the main drive from a neighbouring path, his cape swinging as he walked. I was about to continue on my way when a voice called out, "Hello, Sinclair!"

He came up to me; it was Alfons Beck, the oldest boy

in the boarding-house. I was always glad to see him and I had nothing against him beyond the fact that he was always sarcastic and avuncular with all the junior boys. He was reputed to be as strong as an ox and to have the Headmaster completely under his thumb. He was the hero of many legendary schoolboy episodes.

"What are you doing here?" he shouted affably in the tone the senior boys assumed when they condescended to one of us occasionally ... "Well, I'll bet anything you're writing poetry!"

"Never thought of it," I replied brusquely, repudiating the notion.

He laughed, came closer and chattered in a way to which I had long ceased to be accustomed.

"You don't need to be afraid that I don't understand, Sinclair. There's something about strolling in the evening mist that begets autumn thoughts and one feels in the mood for composing verse, I know. About dying nature, of course, and one's lost youth which is like you. See Heinrich Heine!"

"I'm not as sentimental as that," I objected.

"No offence! But in this weather, I think it's a good idea to look out some spot where there's a glass of wine or something of the sort to be had. Are you coming along? I'm on my own – or would you rather not? I wouldn't want to lead you astray, old man, you might not want to risk getting a black mark!"

Within a short time we were sitting together in a small pub in the suburbs, drinking a doubtful wine and clinking glasses. I did not take to it at all to begin with but at any rate it was something new. Soon however, unaccustomed to wine, I became very loquacious. It was as if a window in me had been broken and the world shone in. It had seemed so long, so terribly long since I had confided anything about my inner self to anyone else. I began to be fanciful and in the middle of it all I told him about the whole Cain and Abel affair.

Beck listened eagerly – here at last was someone to whom I could give something! He slapped me on the back, called me a devil and a sly rogue and my heart swelled with ecstasy at this opportunity of releasing my cooped up longing to speak and communicate, of being recognized and of counting for something with an older boy. When he called me a sly rogue, the words seeped into my soul like a sweet, heady wine. The world glowed in new colours, thoughts gushed out of me like a hundred audacious springs. The fire of enthusiasm burned inside me. We discussed teachers at the school and our school-friends and we seemed to have a perfect understanding of each other. We talked of the Greeks and the pagan world, and Beck was eager to induce me to confess my love affairs. But I was out of my depth. I had had no experience; I had nothing to relate. Moreover the wine failed to release or enable me to communicate whatever I had felt, built up or imagined though I was burning inside. Beck was much more knowledgeable about girls and I listened to his tales with excitement. I heard amazing things; things I would not have thought possible were trotted out as part of everyday reality and seemed quite normal. Alfons Beck had already gained experience of women in his less than eighteen years of life. He had learned, for example, that girls were only out for flirtation and attention, which was all very agreeable but not the real thing. There was more chance of that with mature women. They were much more reasonable. You could talk with Frau Jaggelt who kept the stationer's shop, and a book could not contain all the various goings-on behind her counter.

I sat there spell-bound and stupefied. Certainly I could never have loved Frau Jaggelt – but nevertheless it was terrific. There seemed to be hidden springs, at least for my seniors, whose existence I had never suspected. It all had a false ring about it, a more ordinary and insignificant flavour than love should have, in my opinion, but at all events it was life and adventure and I was sitting next to someone who had actually experienced it and to whom it seemed a normal thing.

Our conversation had now left the heights and had lost its magic. Instead of being the 'bright little fellow,' I had sunk to being a mere boy listening to a man. But all the same – as opposed to what my life had been for months on end, it was, as I gradually began to realize, forbidden fruit; from our presence there in the pub to the subject of our discussion, all very forbidden. In any case it smacked of cleverness and rebellion.

I remember that night with remarkable clarity. It was late when we started on our way home by the wan light of the gas-lamps in the cold, damp night air and I was drunk for the first time in my life. But far from being an agreeable sensation it was extremely distressing and yet even that had a thrill and delightfulness of its own; it was after all rebellion, debauchery, it was life and spirit. Beck boldly took charge of me, cursing me hard at the same time for a 'bloody beginner,' and half led, half carried me home where he managed to bundle first me then himself through an open hall-window.

The sober reality to which I painfully awoke after an all-too brief drunken sleep was accompanied by an unaccountable depression. I sat up in bed, still wearing my everyday shirt; my clothes and shoes lay strewn round about on the floor and reeked of tobacco and vomit, and between fits of headache, nausea and a raging thirst a picture rose before me such as I had long ago ceased to look at. I saw my home, father and mother and sisters and the garden. I saw my quiet, familar bedroom. I saw school and market-place, Demian and the Confirmation classes – everything about it was light, it had an aura of brightness; it was all wonderful, righteous and pure. And everything, as I now realized, that had been mine only yesterday, nay a few hours before and was mine for the asking, had at this very hour, this very moment, depraved and cursed as I was, ceased to belong to me, rejected me, regarded me with disgust. Every act of affection and intimacy which I had experienced in the distant, golden gardens of childhood, every kiss from my mother, every Christmas feast, every bright summer morning at home, every flower in the garden was blighted; I had trampled it all down under foot. If informers had come and tied me up and led me to the gallows as an outcast and defiler of temples, I would have been ready and gone willingly and considered it just and rightful.

So this was how I looked inside! I, who was going round, despising the world! I who was proud in spirit and shared Demian's ideas! That was how I appeared to myself – an outcast, a swine, drunk, besmirched, a vile beast, brought low by my loathsome appetites! That was how I looked to myself, I who had left those gardens where everything was pure, bright, unquestioning affection, I who had loved the music of Bach and beautiful poetry! With mixed feelings of emotion and revulsion I could still hear my own laugh – drunken, uncontrolled, stupid bursts of laughter. That was I!

Yet in spite of it all, I almost revelled in my torment. So long had I crawled along, blind and foolish, for so long had my heart cowered as it were silent and anæmic in a corner, that even this self-reproach, this loathsome feeling was welcome. At least it was emotion of some kind; fire was kindled and my heart raced. Though utterly routed I felt something akin to release and the dawn of spring in the midst of my trouble.

Meantime, seen from without, I was rapidly deteriorating. My initial orgy was soon followed by others. A good deal of tippling and time-wasting went on among my school-fellows. I was one of the youngest among those who misbehaved in this way and I was soon no longer merely a tolerated 'young 'un' but a ringleader and star, a notorious and daring pub-crawler. I belonged once more to the world of darkness, to the Devil and in that world I was considered no end of a lad.

I lived in an orgasm of self-destruction, and while among my friends I was thought of as a devil-may-care leader and a devilishly smart and witty fellow, deep down inside I was full of fear and anxiety. I remember even now that tears sprang to my eyes when I saw children playing in the street one Sunday afternoon as I emerged from a pub, gay and happy with their freshly combed hair and Sunday clothes. And while I often amused and shocked my friends with outrageous cynicism at beer-stained tables, in my inmost heart I was in awe of everything I scoffed at and lay inwardly weeping on my knees before my soul, my past, my mother and God.

There was a good reason why I was never in harmony with my companions and remained lonely among them and suffered because of it. True, I was a drunken hero and mocker after the toughest heart. I displayed spirit and courage in my thoughts and words about my teachers, school, parents and the church – I listened to smutty stories and even ventured on an occasional one myself – but I never accompanied my friends when they went out with girls. I kept to myself and was filled with an intense longing for love, a hopeless longing, while, to judge by my talk, I ought to have been a hardened enjoyer of feminine favours. No one was more outrageous, no one more shameless than I. And when occasionally I saw the young girls of the town walking in front of me, pretty, clean, pleasant and innocent, they seemed like pure wonderful dreams, a thousand times too good and pure for me. For a time I could not even bring myself to enter Frau Jaggelt's stationery shop because it made me blush to look at her, remembering what Alfons Beck had told me.

The more I realized how perpetually lonely and different

from the others I was, the less able was I to break away. I cannot now remember whether my drinking and boasting really gave me any satisfaction. I never became used to drinking to the extent of managing to avoid the disagreeable after-effects on each occasion. It was as if I was compelled to do all these things. I did what I had to because I did not know what to do otherwise. I was afraid of being alone for long and felt nervous when confronted by the many shy and tender impulses which continually attacked me and I was afraid of the thoughts of love that so often surged up in my mind.

What I missed above all was a friend. I had two or three school-mates whom I liked to see. But they belonged to the good types, and my vices had long been an open secret. They avoided me. I was considered as a desperate gambler on the brink of disaster. The teachers knew a good deal about me, I had been severely punished several times and my final expulsion seemed to be merely a matter of time. As I myself knew, I had long ceased to be considered a model pupil, but I forced myself painfully along with the feeling that it could not go on like this for ever.

There are many ways in which providence can make us feel lonely and lead us back to ourselves. Sometimes God seemed to accompany me. It was like a bad dream; I see myself as a dreamer, spellbound, restless and tormented, dragging my odious and unclean way over mud and mire, broken beer glasses and nights filled with cynical chatter. There is the kind of dream in which on your way to the princess you get stuck in quagmires, back lanes full of refuse and foul odours. That was how it was with me. In this rough fashion my loneliness was thrust upon me and I raised, as it were, between myself and my childhood, a locked gateway to Eden with its pitilessly resplendent host of witnesses. It was a beginning, an awakening of nostalgia for my former self.

I had not got rid of my fear. I still had shivering fits as

on the occasion when for the first time, alarmed by my housemaster's letters, my father appeared unexpectedly in St. —— and came to meet me. When towards the end of that winter he paid me a second visit, I was already hardened and indifferent and allowed him to scold and entreat me and remind me of my mother. Finally he grew angry and said that unless I improved he would have me sent away from the school in disgrace and put me in a reformatory. I wished he would! When he went away that time, I pitied him; he had achieved nothing; he could no longer find a way into my heart and for the time being I felt it served him right. I did not care what became of me. In my odd and unattractive way, with my pub visits and outspoken attitude I was at loggerheads with the world at large, and this was the form my protest took. I was ruining myself in the process and sometimes it looked to me as if the world could not find a better use for people like myself. If they could offer no better place, no higher rewards, people like me would come to grief. Well, the loss was the world's.

The Christmas holidays were a joyless affair that year. My mother got into a panic when she saw me again. I had shot up still more and my lean face looked grey and wasted; my features had lost their tautness, my eyes were red-rimmed. My incipient moustache and spectacles, which I had recently acquired, made me look odder still. My sisters recoiled, giggling. It was all very uncomfortable. My conversation with my father in his study was uncomfortable; exchanging greetings with the handful of relations was uncomfortable and above all Christmas itself was an uncomfortable business. Ever since I had lived in our house it had been the great day of festivity and love, gratitude and the renewal of the bond between myself and my parents. This time it was merely oppressive and embarrassing. As usual father read out the passage about the shepherds abiding in the fields 'watching their flocks'; as usual my sisters stood smiling in front of the table on which the Christmas gifts had been placed. But my father's voice sounded displeased and his face looked old and hollow and mother was sad and the atmosphere painful and strained – presents, Christmas wishes, Bible reading and illuminated tree – everything seemed out of place. The gingerbread smelt sweet and evoked a host of more agreeable memories. The Christmas tree with its fragrance reminded me of things as they had been in former days. I longed for Christmas Eve and the holidays to be over.

It was like this the whole winter. Only quite recently I had been solemnly warned by the masters at school and threatened with expulsion. It could not go on much longer. At least as far as I was concerned.

I had one special grudge against Max Demian, whom I had not seen now for some time. I had written to him twice at the beginning of my school term in St. —— but had received no reply; so I had not called on him during the holidays.

In the same park where during the autumn I had met Alfons Beck, in the early spring when the hedges were beginning to show green, I encountered a girl to whom I felt an immediate attraction. I had gone out for a solitary walk, my head filled with unsavoury thoughts and worries, for my health had not been good, and to make matters worse, I was in perpetual financial difficulties. I owed sums of money to various friends and had to keep producing presents by way of bribes, and in several shops I had allowed bills for cigars and suchlike to mount up. Not that these anxieties went very deep – if my existence was to come to an end very soon and I drowned myself or was transferred to a reformatory, these trifling matters would never arise. But I lived face to face with these ugly facts and they made me wretched.

On that spring day in the park, then, I met a young woman. She was tall and slender, smartly dressed and had a boyish face. She attracted me immediately. She belonged to the type I liked and she began to fill my imagination. True, she was not much older than I but much more mature. She was elegant and well-formed, already a grown woman but with a touch of exuberant boyishness in her face which made a particular appeal to me.

So far in my life I had never managed to approach a girl with whom I was in love nor did I succeed on the present occasion. But the incident made a deeper impression on me than anything before, and this infatuation had a profound influence on my life.

Once more an image had suddenly risen up before me, a lofty and respected image – alas, nothing could have been deeper and stronger within me than my craving for someone to worship and respect. I called her Beatrice for I knew about her, without having read Dante, from the reproduction of an English painting I had kept. It showed a young pre-Raphaelite woman, long-limbed and slender with a narrow head and refined hands and features. My beautiful girl was not quite like her although she had the same slenderness and boyish figure which attracted me and something of her intellectual or spiritual expression.

I never spoke a single word to Beatrice, yet at that time she had the profoundest influence on me. Her image stood before me, like a holy altar. She transformed me into someone praying in a temple. Day after day I avoided drinking and other nocturnal expeditions. I could be alone again, enjoy reading and going for walks.

My sudden conversion drew plenty of mockery down on my head. But now I had an object for my love, someone to look up to. Once again I had an ideal; life once more was full of mystery, gaiety, mysterious twilight, and I felt at ease again and at home even if only as the servant and slave of an honoured image.

Once more I was trying with all my might to reconstruct my 'world of light' out of the ruins of a devastated portion of my life; once more I lived for the sole aim of getting rid of the darkness and evil within me and regaining the world of light, on my knees before God. This 'world of light' continued to be to some extent my own creation; it was no longer an escape, a means of crawling back to the shelter of my mother and irresponsible security. It was a new service, one I myself had discovered and desired. The sexuality which was a torment from which I was continually in flight was now transfigured into spirituality and devotion in this holy fire. There would be no more darkness, nothing hateful, no more tortured nights, no excitement in front of lascivious pictures, no eavesdropping at forbidden doors, no lewdness. In place of all this I raised my altar with the image of Beatrice, and in dedicating myself to her, I was dedicating myself to the holy spirit and the gods, sacrificing the portion of my life which I had withdrawn from the powers of darkness to the powers of light. My goal became purity, not pleasure; happiness was replaced by beauty and spirituality.

This cult of Beatrice completely changed my life. The precocious cynic of yesterday had become an acolyte and I set my heart on becoming a saint. Not only did I cast off the evil life to which I had become accustomed but I sought to transform myself utterly, to introduce purity, nobility and worthiness into everything; my thoughts were fixed on this aim while I ate, drank, talked and dressed. I began the day with cold baths which cost me a great effort. I bore myself in a dignified and serious manner, carried myself stiffly and assumed a slow, solemn gait which must have looked comic to outsiders but to me it was merely an act of worship.

Of all the new practices in which I sought to express my new mood, one had become all-important. I began to paint. It arose from the fact that the English portrait of Beatrice which I possessed was not enough like the girl of my heart. I wanted to try and paint her portrait for myself. With a new feeling of joy and hope I took into the room – I had recently acquired one of my own – some good drawing-paper, colours and a paint brush and prepared my palette, glass, porcelain dish and pencils. The fine tempera colours in small tubes which I had bought delighted me. Among them was a fiery chrome green and I can still see today how its colour flashed at me for the first time in the little white dish.

I began carefully.. Portraiture was beyond my powers: I wanted to start with something else and so I painted ornaments, flower pieces and small, imaginative landscape compositions, a tree beside a chapel, a Roman bridge with cypress trees. I often became completely immersed in this game and was as happy as a child with his paint-box. Finally I began on my portrait of Beatrice.

I spoilt a number of sheets of paper and threw them away. The more I endeavoured to capture the features of the girl whom I occasionally encountered in the street, the less successful I was. Finally I gave up the attempt and contented myself with painting a face from my imagination and ideas that arose spontaneously as I dipped my brush in the paint. It was a dream-face that emerged and I was not satisfied with it. Yet I persisted with the experiment, and with every new sketch approached the type more nearly even if it was still far removed from reality.

I grew more and more accustomed to drawing lines idly with my pencil and colouring areas, without any model in mind except whatever found its way on to the paper from my subconscious and took shape in these half-serious scrawls.

At length one day, almost without knowing, I produced a portrait which expressed something more definite than the previous ones. It was not the face of the girl; it had long ceased to be that but something quite different, unreal, yet it meant just as much to me. It looked more like a boy's head than a girl's; the hair was not flaxen like my pretty girl's but chestnut with a tinge of red; the chin was strong and determined, the lips rosy; the whole was rather stiff and mask-like but it was impressive and hinted at a secret inner life.

I became conscious of a strange impression as I sat before the completed picture. It resembled a kind of god-image or sacred mask, half-male, half-female, ageless, purposeful yet dreamy, frozen yet mysteriously alive. This face had some message for me; it belonged to me; it was making some demand. It was like someone, but I could not decide whom.

This picture haunted my thoughts for a long time and divided up my life. I kept it hidden away in a drawer; no one should lay hands on it and make use of it to mock me. But as soon as I was in my own small room, I pulled it out and communed with it. In the evening I nailed it on to the wall, facing my bed, gazed on it until I fell asleep, and it was the first object my eyes opened onto in the morning.

It was precisely at that time that I began having a great many dreams again as I had done during my childhood. I felt as if I had not dreamed before for years. Now a new kind of picture appeared before me; time after time the painted portrait arose, living, eloquent, friendly or hostile, sometimes distorted, sometimes beautiful, harmonious and noble.

Then one morning when I awoke from one of these dreams, I suddenly recognized it. It looked so fantastically familiar and seemed to call out my name. It appeared to know me as a mother, as if its eyes had been fixed on me all my life.

I stared at the picture with beating heart, the close, brown hair, the half-feminine mouth, the strong forehead with its strange brightness – which it had assumed of its own accord – and I realized that my recognition, my rediscovery and knowledge of it were becoming more and more a reality.

I leapt out of bed, stood before the face and, from close range, looked into the wide-open, greenish, staring eyes, the right one of which was slightly higher than the other. All at once the right eye seemed to twitch, faintly but unmistakeably and I was able to recognize the portrait . . .

Why had it only just dawned on me! It was Demian's face.

Later I often compared the face on the paper with Demian's features as I remembered them. They were certainly, though similar, not the same. But beyond all doubt, it was Demian.

Once one evening in early summer the sun was slanting red through my window that faced westward. Inside the room it was dusk. It occurred to me to attach the picture of Beatrice (or Demian) to the window bar and watch the effect as the sun shone through. The outlines of the face were blurred but the eyes, edged with pink, the brightness of the forehead and the energetic red mouth glowed excitingly from the surface. For a long time I sat opposite it even after the picture had faded out. And gradually a feeling came over me that it was neither Beatrice nor Demian but myself. Not that the picture was like me – I did not feel it should be – but the face somehow expressed my life, it was my inner self, my fate or my daimon. That was how my friend would look if and when I ever found him again. The woman I loved, if ever I had a lover, would look like that. It was the pattern of my life and death; it expressed the tone and rhythm of my fate.

During those weeks I had embarked on some reading which made a deeper impression on me than anything I had read before. Even in later life I have seldom been so completely absorbed by any books, perhaps not even excepting Nietzsche's. It was a volume of Novalis* con-

*Translator's note. The novel Demian was first published under the pseudonym Emil Sinclair, the name of a friend of the poet Novalis whom Hesse so much admired.

taining letters and sayings, many of which I did not understand and all of which attracted and excited me in an unaccountable fashion. One of the sayings occurred to me at that moment. I picked up my pen and wrote it under the picture, "Fate and temperament are the names of a concept." Now I understood.

I frequently met the girl I called Beatrice but these encounters did not move me any more; I was merely aware of an uninterrupted harmony and a sympathetic longing which said: you are bound up with me, not you yourself but your image; you are part of my fate.

My longing for Max Demian overwhelmed me again. I had had no news of him for years. I had met him on one single occasion in the holidays. I now see that I made no mention of that brief meeting in my notes and realize that it was out of shame and vanity that I suppressed the allusion. I must fill this gap.

Thus, one day in the holidays when I was strolling through my home town wearing my blasé, perpetually weary pub-crawling expression, swinging my stick and staring into the old, despised, unchanging faces of the townsfolk, my former friend advanced towards me. A shudder ran through me almost as soon as I set eyes on him. My thoughts flashed back to Franz Kromer. Could Demian have really forgotten that business? It was so disagreeable to feel that indebtedness to him – just for a mere stupid childish episode, but it was a debt all the same . . .

He appeared to be waiting to see if I would greet him and when I did, as casually as possible, he stretched out his hand. He gave me his old grip; firm, warm and yet cool and virile.

He scrutinized my face and said, "You've grown up, Sinclair." He himself seemed quite unchanged, as old and as young as ever. He joined me and we went for a walk and exchanged idle nothings. Not a word was said about the old days. It occurred to me that I had written to him several times in the past without receiving a reply. I hoped he had forgotten those stupid, stupid letters! He made no mention of them.

At that time I had not come across Beatrice and there was no portrait. I was still in the middle of my period of depression. When we reached the outskirts of the town, I invited him to come into a pub. He did so. Boastfully I ordered a bottle of wine, handed him a glass, clinked my glass with his and demonstrated my familiarity with student customs. I emptied the first glass at one gulp.

"Do you often visit the pub?" he asked.

"Oh yes," I replied casually, "what else is there to do? After all it's the most cheerful way of spending one's time."

"Do you think so? It may well be. There's certainly a pleasant element in it – the carouse, Bacchanalian revels! But that is just what the majority of people who spend a lot of time in pubs miss. It seems to me that this pub-haunting is a very humdrum affair. A whole night with blazing torches for a proper carousal and riot, yes! But this continual business, one glass after another, it doesn't appear to me the real thing. Can you imagine Faust sitting at a pub table night after night?"

I drank my wine and gave him a hostile look.

"No, but everybody isn't Faust," I replied curtly.

He looked at me somewhat perplexed.

"Oh well, it's not worth arguing about. Anyhow, the life of a soaker or wastrel is, one supposes, more lively than that of the blameless citizen. And then – I once read it somewhere – the life of the wastrel is the best preparation for the mystic. There are men such as Saint Augustine who became saints. Previously he had been a hedonist and man of the world."

I felt mistrustful and had no wish to defer to him and so I said in a blasé voice, "Yes, everyone to his taste. But I must admit frankly that it wouldn't interest me to turn saint or anything of that sort."

Demian darted a shrewd glance at me from his half-closed eyes.

"My dear Sinclair," he drawled, "I wasn't trying to say anything to upset you. At all events, neither of us knows what your aim is in putting back this wine. Only that part of you that composes your life can know. It is good to know that we have within us one who knows everything about us, wills everything, does everything better than we can ourselves. But you must excuse me, I must be off home."

We exchanged a brief goodbye. I sat down disgruntled, drank up the contents of my bottle and discovered when I rose to go that Demian had already paid, which annoyed me still further.

My thoughts returned once more to that slight incident. I could not forget him. And the words he had said in that tavern in the suburbs came back to my mind, strangely fresh and significant. "It is good to know that we have within us one who knows everything about us!"

I glanced at the picture which hung in the window and had now almost faded out. But I could see that the eyes were still glowing. It was Demian's look or else it was he who was inside me; he knew everything about me.

How I longed for Demian! I knew nothing about him; he was beyond my reach. All I knew was that he was probably studying and that he, once his schooldays were over, had left his mother and his native town.

I made an effort to assemble all my recollections of Max Demian up to the period of the Kromer incident. How much of what he had once said to me still echoed in my ears, still held a meaning for me today and touched me closely. Even what he had said about the wastrel and saint on our last, unhappy meeting suddenly rose clearly before me. Was not that how it had been with me? Had I not lived in an atmosphere of tippling and squalor, lost and half in a daze, until with a new zest for life there had been a complete transformation within me and a longing for purity, a craving for saintliness?

And so I pursued these memories; it had long been night and it was raining outside. Even through my recollections I could hear it raining; there had been that time under the chestnut trees where he had once questioned me about Franz Kromer and had guessed the first secrets of my life. One thing had followed another – our conversations on our way to school, the confirmation classes. Finally I recalled my first meeting with Max Demian. What had we talked about? I could not remember at first but I waited and remained plunged in thought. Then that came back too. We had been standing in front of our house after he had voiced his opinions about the Cain story. Next he had spoken about the old, half-faded coat-of-arms on the keystone above our front entrance. He had said that it interested him, and that one should take a note of such things.

That night I dreamed of Demian and the coat-of-arms. It kept changing. Demian held it in his hands; sometimes it was small and grey, sometimes large and multicoloured, but he explained to me that it was always the same bird. Finally, however, he ordered me to eat the coat-of-arms. When I had swallowed it, I realized in a terrible panic that the heraldic bird I had swallowed was inside me, swelling out and was beginning to devour me from within. Full of a deadly fear, I awoke with a start.

I was wide awake; it was the middle of the night and I could hear the rain entering into the room. I got up to close the window and in the process stood on something bright that lay on the floor. Next morning, I found it was my painted sheet of paper. It lay on the wet floor and had curled up. I spread it out to dry in a heavy book between two sheets of blotting paper. When I looked at it next day, it had dried but it had changed. The red lips had faded and contracted a little. They now looked exactly like Demian's.

I set about painting a fresh picture – the heraldic bird. I can no longer remember exactly what the result was like but there was one thing, as I knew, which could no longer be made out in the original even close to since the thing was old and had often been repainted. The bird was standing or perched on some object – it might have been a flower, a basket, a nest or a tree-top. I could not be bothered about that and I began on the part which I could clearly visualize. At the promptings of some vague urge I immediately started by employing strong colours, painting the bird's head a golden yellow on my paper. I continued as the mood took me and completed the whole within a few days.

It now represented a bird of prey with a narrow and cruel sparrow-hawk head. Half its body was sunk in a dark, terrestrial globe and from this it was struggling to disengage itself as from a giant egg, against a background of blue sky. The longer I examined the sheet, the more it was borne in upon me that it was the coloured coat-of-arms as it had appeared in my dream.

It would have been impossible for me to write to Demian even if I had known where to address the letter. But I resolved to send him the picture of the sparrow-hawk with the same dreamy clairvoyance with which I did everything – irrespective of whether it would ever reach him. I did not write anything on it – not even my name, trimmed the edges carefully, bought a large envelope and wrote my friend's old address on it and despatched it.

An examination time was approaching and I had to do more school work than usual. The masters had reinstated me in favour since my sudden conversion from my previous, despicable mode of life. Not that I was now by any means a model pupil, but neither I nor anyone else could have imagined that only six months before everybody had considered my expulsion in disgrace extremely likely.

My father now wrote to me in his old vein, free from reproach and threat. Yet I felt no impulse to explain to him or to anyone else how the transformation had been effected in me. It was chance that this conversion coincided with my parents' and teachers' wishes. But it did not bring me any closer to the others or indeed to anyone; it merely increased my loneliness. For my reformation had only the vaguest target, Demian, in the far-distant future. I did not even know myself; I was too much involved. Beatrice had been the starting-point, but for some time I had been living with my painted pictures and my thoughts of Demian in a world so unreal that it was completely lost both to my sight and mind. I could never have brought myself to breathe a word to anyone else about my dreams, my aspirations and my inner transformation even if I had wanted to.

But how could I have wanted to?

V The Bird Struggles Out of the Egg

My painted dream-bird was on its way in search of my friend. In what seemed a miraculous fashion a reply had reached me.

I was in the classroom during the break between two lessons and on my desk I found a piece of paper tucked in my book. It was folded in the customary way we had for the notes we wrote to each other during class. My sole surprise was as to who could be sending me a note of that kind, for I was not on that sort of relationship with any of my school-fellows. I thought it would turn out to be an invitation to take part in some school rag in which I would refuse to be involved, and I placed the paper unread in front of my book. It was not until the lesson had started that the note found its way back into my hand.

I fidgeted with the paper, unfolded it casually and saw that it contained a few words. I glanced at them; a phrase pulled me up short; I panicked and read on, my heart contracted in cold fear before my fate. "The bird is struggling out of the egg," it read. "The egg is the world. Whoever wants to be born must first destroy a world. The bird is flying to God. The name of the God is called Abraxas."

After reading over these lines several times, I sank into a deep reverie. There was no room for any doubt; it was Demian's reply. No one except he and I knew about the bird. My picture had reached him. He had understood and was endeavouring to enlighten me. But what was the connection? And – this was what troubled me most – what was this Abraxas? I had never heard or read the word. "The name of the God is called Abraxas."

The lesson passed by without my taking in a word of it.

The next began, the last in the afternoon. It was taken by a young assistant master who had just come down from the university. We liked him because he was so young and did not assume any false dignity when dealing with us.

We were doing Herodotus under this Dr. Follen's guidance. This reading period was one of the few items in the curriculum that interested me. But on this occasion I was far away. I had opened my book mechanically in front of me but was not following the translation. I was deeply immersed in my own thoughts. Furthermore I had on several occasions tested the correctness of Demian's remark made to me during a scripture lesson in the old days. If you wanted something strongly enough, you achieved it.

Thus when I was very preoccupied with my own thoughts during a lesson, I could be quite quiet and the master would leave me undisturbed. True, if you were inattentive or sleepy you would suddenly find him standing by you – that had happened to me already. But if you were really thinking, really absorbed, you were protected. I had also experimented with the staring-out technique and had found it effective. In Demian's time I had not pulled it off but now I realized that one could bring about a great deal just by thinking and intensive staring.

So I was sitting now miles away from Herodotus and school when the master's voice made a sudden impact on my consciousness like a thunderbolt, and I woke up in a panic. I could hear his voice; he stood close to me; I thought he had already called out my name. But he did not look at me. I breathed again.

Then I heard his voice again. I heard it saying loudly the word "Abraxas."

In the course of an explanation, the beginning of which had escaped me, Dr. Follen continued, "We must not imagine the views of those sects and mystical societies of antiquity to be as ingenuous as they at first sight appear from a rational consideration. Science as we know it was absolutely unknown to antiquity. They compensated for this by their preoccupation with philosophical and mystical truths which were very highly developed. From this arose a kind of black magic that often led to error and crime. But this magic had also noble antecedents and was based on a certain profundity of thought. The teaching of Abraxas, for example, which I cited to you a moment ago. This name was mentioned in connection with magic Greek formulas and it was often considered to be the name of some evil spirit of the kind that some uncivilized tribes still believe in today. It appears, however, that Abraxas has a much deeper significance. We can therefore think of the name as one of a godhead who symbolizes the reconciliation of the godly and the satanic."

The learned little man spoke with eagerness and intelligence but no one was very attentive and as the name did not recur in the text my attention wandered off to my own affairs.

"Reconcile the godly and the satanic." The words provoked an echo inside me. I remembered the connection. The idea had been mentioned to me by Demian in the course of a conversation with him during the last days of our friendship. On that occasion Demian had said that we had indeed a god whom we honoured but he represented only one half of the world purposely separated, that is to say the official, authorised 'world of light.' But we ought to be able to honour the whole world and so we must have either *one* god who was also devil or side by side with the cult of God we should institute a cult of the Devil. So we had Abraxas the god who was both God and Devil.

For a time I eagerly pursued this clue without, however, getting any further. I unsuccessfully ransacked a whole library for references to Abraxas but I could never be more than half-hearted in this kind of direct, conscious research in which one can only find truths that are so much dead weight.

The form of Beatrice which had so earnestly preoccupied me for some time was gradually being submerged or was slowly drifting away from me, moving further and further away towards the horizon, becoming paler, more shadowy and remote. It no longer satisfied my inner being.

A new image now began to take shape in the strange, withdrawn existence which I was leading like a sleep-walker. The longing for life began to blossom out in me, the longing for love deepened and the sex urge which I had been able to sublimate for a time in my adoration of Beatrice now demanded a new set of images and new objectives. But these wishes remained unfulfilled, and it became more impossible than ever for me to modify this longing and expect anything from the girls among whom my friends sought their happiness. I dreamed vividly again and more in fact in day-time than at night. Fancies and images or desires rose up before me and drew me away from the exterior world so that I had more substantial and active dealings with those fancies, dreams and shadows, and dwelt among them more than in the world of reality around me.

One definite dream or fantasy which kept recurring struck me as particularly significant. This dream, the most important and enduring of my life, followed this pattern: I was on my way to my parents' home and over the main entrance the heraldic bird gleamed gold on an azure ground. My mother walked towards me but when I entered and she was about to kiss me, it was no longer she but a form I had never set eyes on, tall and strong with a look of Max Demian and my painted portrait – yet it was somehow different and despite the robust frame, very feminine. The form drew me to itself and enveloped me in a deep, shuddering embrace. My feelings were a mixture of ecstasy and horror, the embrace was at once an act of worship and a crime. The form that embraced me had something about it of both my mother and my friend Demian and also this embrace violated every sense of religious awe, yet it was bliss. Sometimes I awoke out of this dream with a feeling of ecstasy, sometimes in mortal fear and with a tortured conscience as if I had committed some terrible sin.

Only gradually and unconsciously was a link being forged between this wholly inner image and the 'sign' that came to me from outside concerning the god I had to search for. The link then grew closer and more intimate, and I began to feel that in this dream of longing I was invoking Abraxas himself. Ecstasy and horror, a mixture of male and female, an intertwining of the sacred and profane, flashes of profound guilt in the most tender innocence – such was the nature of my love-fantasy, such was Abraxas. Love had ceased to be the dark animal urge I had first experienced with misgiving nor was it the piously spiritualized cult I had brought to the image of Beatrice. It was both and a good deal more besides; it was the image of angels and the Devil, man and woman, human being and beast, highest good and the worst evil. It seemed that I was ordained to live in this fashion, that this was my fate. My craving for it was not untinged with fear but there was no escape; it hovered over me continually.

Next spring I was to leave school and proceed with more advanced studies but I was still undecided as to where and what I was to study. A faint down had appeared on my upper lip. I was a grown man and yet completely helpless and without purpose. Only one thing persisted, the inner voice, the dream-image. I felt it was my duty to follow blindly wherever this vision might lead me. But it was not easy and every day I rejected it afresh.

Perhaps, as I often thought, I was mad; perhaps merely different from other men. But I too could do what others did; with a little effort and industry I could read Plato, solve problems of trigonometry or understand chemical analyses. There was only one thing I could not do – wrest from myself the darkly hidden goal and obtain some sort of picture – as others did who knew exactly that they wanted to become teachers, judges, doctors or artists – of how long the process would take and what hopes such a future could hold out. But this I could not do. Perhaps it would be possible one day, but could I feel assured of that? Perhaps I should have to seek continually for years and then become nothing; I would attain some goal but it would be an evil, dangerous and fearful one.

All I wanted was to try and realize whatever was in me. Why was that so difficult?

I made frequent attempts to paint the forceful dream-apparition but always without success. If I had been successful I would have sent the picture to Demian. Where was he? I did not know. I only knew that our fates were bound up together. When would I see him again?

The pleasant tranquillity of the weeks and months of the Beatrice period had long receded. At that time I had thought I had reached an island and found peace at last. But it was always like that – practically no situation seemed agreeable. I was no sooner cheered by a dream than it immediately faded. It was no use moaning for it! I now had within me a furnace of unsatisfied cravings, a tense expectancy which often made me completely wild and mad. I often saw the dream apparition before me, miraculously clear, clearer than my own hand, spoke with it, wept before it, cursed it. I called it mother and knelt before it in tears; I called it devil and whore, vampire and murderer. It enticed me into the gentlest dreams of love and barren shamelessness; nothing was too good and precious, nothing too wicked or vile.

I passed the whole of that winter in a state of inner turbulence which I find difficult to describe. I had been long accustomed to loneliness; it did not oppress me for

I was living with Demian, with the sparrow-hawk, with the image of the great dream-form which was both my fate and my beloved. And it provided for all the needs of my life since everything was directed towards greatness and space – it all pointed towards Abraxas. Yet none of these dream pictures came at my bidding; I could not summon any of them, I could not, at will, give any one of them its colours. It was they who took me; I was governed and lived by them.

I was well armed against the outside world. I had no fear of men; I had learned that lesson from my schoolfellows who treated me with a secret respect which often brought a smile to my lips. When I so desired I could see very clearly through most of them and astonish them on occasion. But seldom if ever did I wish to do so. I was solely and exclusively preoccupied with my inner self. I wanted to live for a while longer in order to give something of myself to the world, to grapple and do battle with it. Many a time when I went through the streets in the evening and my restlessness prevented me from returning home before midnight, I felt convinced that my 'beloved' was bound to meet me, pass me at the next corner, call to me from the nearest window. Often it all seemed unendurable and I resolved to put an end to my life.

Just then I found a strange refuge – by chance as they say – though I believe there is no such thing. When a person urgently needs something and finds what he requires, it is not chance that gives him it, it is himself, his own craving and urgency that bring it to him.

On two or three occasions then during my walks through the town I had heard an organ in a small church in the suburbs without stopping to listen. The next time I was passing I heard it again and recognized that it was Bach. I approached the church door which I found to be locked and as the street was almost deserted, I sat down by the church on a curbstone, turned up my coat-collar and listened. It was a small but good organ and it was being marvellously played with a peculiar and extremely individual expressiveness of will and determination which gave the impression of a prayer. The player, I thought, knows that a treasure is hidden in this music; he woos it, knocks at the door, wrestles for this treasure as he would for his life. My knowledge of music is very limited technically but from childhood onwards I have had an intuitive grasp of such music of the soul and experienced it as something inevitable.

The organist played something more modern afterwards; it might have been by Max Reger. The church was completely dark; only a very thin gleam of light penetrated the nearest window. I waited until the music had stopped and strolled up and down until I saw the organist emerge. He was still quite young but older than I was, short and squat, and he moved off quickly with energetic yet somehow reluctant strides.

On many occasions after that I sat by the church or walked up and down outside at the evening hour and once found the door open and sat for half an hour in a pew, frozen yet contented while the organist above my head played in the dim gaslight. It was not the music he was playing that I heard but himself; there seemed to be a relationship and secret connection between all the things he played. Everything was devotional, consecrated and devout but not devout after the manner that churchgoers and pastors are; but devout like the pilgrims and mendicants in the Middle Ages; devout with that careless surrender to a feeling of universality which transcends all knowledge. The organist gave renderings of the masters who preceded Bach and of old Italian masters. They all said the same thing, they all expressed what the musician had in his soul – longing, inner understanding of the world and at the same time the wildest separation from it, a burning hearkening to the deep places of the soul, intoxication of religious devotion and deep curiosity about the miraculous.

Once when I followed the organist unobserved on his way out of the church, I saw him enter a small tavern at the outskirts of the town. I could not resist the urge to go in after him. Now, for the first time, I had a clear view of him. He was sitting at the host's table in a corner of the parlour, a black felt hat on his head, a glass of wine in front of him, and his face was just what I had anticipated. It was ugly and somewhat wild looking, interrogative and erratic, wayward and obstinate yet the mouth had something soft and childish about it. All the masculinity and strength was in the eyes and brow; the lower half of his face was tender and immature, indecisive and to some extent feminine; the chin, irresolute, boylike, contradicted the forehead and expression. What I liked were the dark brown eyes full of pride and hostility.

I sat down opposite to him without a word; there was nobody else in the inn. He flashed a glance at me as if he wanted to get rid of me. But I held it and stared back unmoved until he shouted in a peevish tone, "Why are you looking at me so devilishly hard? Do you want something out of me?"

"No, I don't want anything from you," I replied, "but I have already had a good deal."

He knitted his brows.

"So you're a music enthusiast? I think it's revolting to be mad about music."

But I refused to be intimidated.

"I have often listened to you in the church over there," I said. "But I won't importune you further. I thought I should perhaps discover something about you, something special, I don't really know what. But perhaps you would rather not listen to me! I can always listen to *you* in church."

"But I always lock it!"

"Just recently you forgot to, and I sat inside. Otherwise

I stand outside or sit on the curb."

"Oh! Another time you may come in, it's warmer. All you've got to do is to knock at the door. But bang hard and not while I'm playing. But fire ahead – what do you want to tell me? You're a young fellow, probably a schoolboy or university student. Are you a musician?"

"No, I like listening but only to the kind of music you play, pure music, the music that makes you feel that someone is shaking heaven and hell. I am fond of music I think because it is so amoral. Everything else is moral and I am after something that isn't. I have always found moralizing intolerable. I don't know how to put it. Do you realize that there must be a god who is both God and Devil? There's supposed to be one, I've heard about it."

The musician pushed his hat back on his head and tossed his hair back, away from his lofty forehead. At the same time he gave me a piercing glance and nodded to me across the table.

In a gentle, eager voice he asked, "What is the name of the god of whom you speak?"

"Unfortunately I know practically nothing about him except his name which is Abraxas."

The musician gave a vaguely mistrustful glance round him as though someone might be spying on us. Then he bent over to me and whispered. "I thought as much. Who are you?"

"I'm a pupil at the grammar school."

"How do you know about Abraxas?"

"Just by chance."

He struck the table so that the wine spilled out of his glass.

"Chance! Don't talk rubbish, young fellow! One doesn't get to know about Abraxas by chance, mark my words. I'll tell you more about him. I know a little."

He fell silent and pushed his chair back. When I looked expectantly at him, he pulled a face.

"Not here! Another time. Here, take some!"

So saying he delved into the pocket of his overcoat which he had not removed and pulled out a handful of roast chestnuts which he threw over to me.

I said nothing, took them and ate them and felt very happy.

"Well," he whispered after a while. "How do you know about – him?"

I did not hesitate to tell him.

"I was alone and desperate at the time," I said. "Then a friend of my earlier days intervened who knows, I think, a good deal about him. I had painted something, a bird emerging from a terrestrial globe which I sent to him. Some time later when I had really forgotten about it, I received a slip of paper on which this was written, 'The bird is struggling out of the egg. The egg is the world. Whoever wants to be born must destroy a world. The bird is flying to God. The name of the God is called Abraxas.' "

He did not reply; we shelled our chestnuts and ate them with the wine.

"What about another glass?" he asked.

"No thank you. I'm not keen on drinking."

He gave a slightly disappointed laugh.

"As you will! It's quite the reverse with me. I'll stay here, but you go along now!"

The next time I went with him after the organ music, he was not very communicative. He led me down an old lane and up the stairs of a stately old house into a large, somewhat gloomy and neglected room where apart from the piano there was nothing to suggest music; on the other hand a large bookcase and writing desk gave the room a studious look.

"What a quantity of books you have," I remarked as I took them in.

"Part of them come from my father's library; I live

with him – Yes, I reside with my father and mother but I cannot introduce you to them because my acquaintances are not greatly respected in this house. I am a Prodigal Son, you know. My father is terribly respectable, an important pastor and preacher in this town. And, for your information, I must tell you that I am his talented and promising son who has gone astray and to some extent even mad. I was a theology student and left that honourable faculty shortly before the State Examination. Though I still retain my interest in the subject as far as my private studies are concerned. What sort of gods people devised for themselves in the old days I still consider an important and fascinating study. Furthermore I am a musician now and I am shortly to obtain some insignificant appointment as an organist, so it seems. Then I shall be back in the Church again."

I glanced along the spines of the books, noticed Greek, Latin and Hebrew titles as far as the feeble light from the small table-lamp permitted. Meantime my acquaintance had lain down on the floor in the darkness and appeared to be preparing for something.

"Come," he called out after a time, "we will now practise a little philosophy. That means holding our tongues, lying on our bellies and thinking."

He struck a match and set light to the paper and wood in the fireplace in front of which he was sprawling. The flames leapt high; he poked and fed them with exaggerated care. I lay next to him on the threadbare carpet. He stared into the fire which attracted me too and we lay on our bellies a good hour in front of the flickering log fire, watching the flames dart about, sink, curve and flicker and finally die down in a quiet sunken glow in the hearth.

"Fire-worship was by no means the most stupid invention," he muttered once to himself. Apart from this, neither of us said a word. I stared hard into the fire, sank into a tranquil reverie, saw shapes in the smoke and pictures in the ashes. Once I started up. My companion was throwing a piece of rosin into the red-hot embers; a small, slender flame shot up and I saw in it the bird with the yellow sparrow hawk's head. In the dying embers threads of gold wove nets, letters of the alphabet and pictures appeared, hints of faces, animals, plant-forms, worms and snakes. When I awoke from my reverie and looked at my friend he was gazing with fanatical concentration into the ashes, his chin resting on his fists.

"I must go now," I murmured.

"Go then, goodbye!"

He did not rise to his feet and as the lamp was out, I had to grope my way out of the cursed old house through dark rooms and corridors. I stopped in the street and looked up at the old house. There was no light burning in any one of the windows. A small brass plate on the front-door gleamed in the light from the gas-lamp. On it I read the words, "Pistorius, rector."

Not until I got home and was sitting alone in my little room after supper did it occur to me that I had heard nothing either about Abraxas or Pistorius and that we had scarcely exchanged half a dozen words. But I was very satisfied with my visit. And for our next meeting he had promised to play me an exquisite piece of ancient organ music, a passacaglia by Buxtehude.

Without realizing it, the organist, Pistorius, had given me my first lesson when I had lain beside him in front of the fire on the floor of his hermit's room. Staring into the fire had done me good; it had strengthened and confirmed certain predispositions which I had always possessed but never cultivated. Gradually I was beginning to understand them.

Even as a child I had had at intervals a fondness for observing strange forms in nature, not so much examining them as surrendering myself to their magic, their oblique message. Long tree-roots, coloured veins in rock, patches of oil floating on water, flaws in glass – all such things had a certain fascination for me, above all, water and fire, smoke, clouds, dust and especially the swirling specks of colour which swam before my closed eyes. In the days following my first visit to Pistorius, I began to call all this to mind. For I noticed that I owed a new strength and gaiety, an intensification of feeling – of which I only became aware later – exclusively to this prolonged staring into the fire. I found it remarkably comforting and rewarding.

To the few experiences which I had so far discovered on the road to my goal was now added this new one. The consideration of such images as I have mentioned, the surrender to odd, irrational forms in nature produces in us a sense of the harmony of our inner being with the will which has been responsible for these shapes. Soon we become aware of the temptation to think of them as being our own moods, our own creations; we see the boundaries between ourselves and nature quiver and dissolve and we become acquainted with the state of mind when we are unable to decide whether the lineaments of our body result from impressions received from outside or from within us. In no other practice is it so simple to discover how creative we are and to what extent our souls participate in the continuous creation of the world. To an even greater extent it is this same indivisible divinity which is active in us and in nature so that if the outer world were destroyed each one of us would be capable of building it up again. For mountain and stream, tree and leaf, root and blossom, every form in nature is echoed in us and originates in the soul whose being is eternity and is hidden from us but none the less gives itself to us for the most part in the power of love and creation.

It was not until many years later that I found this view recorded in a book by Leonardo da Vinci who on one occasion describes how good and deeply moving it is to look at a wall which many people have spat upon. Confronted with each stain on the wet wall, he must have felt the same as Pistorius and I did in front of the fire.

At our next meeting the organist offered an explanation. "We always set too narrow limits on our personalities. We count as ours merely what we experience differently as individuals or recognize as being divergent. Yet we consist of the whole existence of the world, each one of us, and just as our body bears in it the various stages of our evolution back to the fish and further back still, we have in our soul everything that has ever existed in the human mind. All the gods and devils whether among the Greeks, Chinese or Zulus are all within us, existing as possibilities, wishes, outlets. If the human race dwindled to one single, half-developed child that had received no education, this child would rediscover the entire course of evolution, would be able to produce gods, devils, paradise, commandments and interdictions, the whole of the Old and New Testament, everything."

"It's all very well," I interpolated, "but what then is the value of the individual? Why do we still struggle on if everything is already complete within us?"

"Stop!" cried Pistorius peremptorily. "There is a great deal of difference between bearing the world within you and being conscious of that piece of knowledge. A madman can produce thoughts that are an echo of Plato and a pious young schoolboy in a theological college ponders on profound mythological connections which occur in the Gnostics or Zoroaster. But he knows nothing of it! While he remains ignorant he is a tree or a stone, at best an animal. Once however he has the first glimmering of this knowledge he becomes a man. You do not think of all the bipeds who walk along the street as human beings merely because they walk upright and carry their young nine months! You can see how many of them are fish or sheep, worms or angels, how many are ants, how many are bees! Human potentialities are present in each one of them but only when he realizes them and learns to make them to some extent a conscious part of him, can the individual be said to possess them."

Such was the general tenor of our conversations together. Rarely did they teach me anything completely new or bring me any overwhelming surprises. They all, however, even the most banal, struck a gentle but continuous hammer-blow on the same spot inside me; they helped to shape me, to peel off my layers of skin, break the egg-shells, and as I emerged from each stage I raised my head a little higher with a greater feeling of freedom until my yellow bird pushed his handsome predatory head out of the shattered shell of the terrestrial globe.

We frequently recounted our dreams to each other and Pistorius was able to provide an interpretation. I even recall one remarkable example. I had a dream in which I was able to fly yet only in such a manner that I was somehow flung into the air, and yet had no mastery over it. The sensation of this flight was exhilarating but it soon turned into fear when I saw myself, powerless, flung to a considerable height. I then made the comforting discovery that I could regulate my rise and fall by holding or releasing my breath.

Pistorius explained it to me; "The impetus which enables you to fly is our great human possession. Everybody has it. It is the feeling of the connection one has with every source of power. But it is frightening! It is devilishly dangerous! That is why the majority of people are so willing to renounce any idea of flying and prefer to stroll quietly along the pavement and obey the law. But you are not one of these. You have higher aspirations as behoves a man of spirit. And look! You discover the miracle that you are gradually winning the mastery and that to the great common power which sweeps you upward is added a fine, subtle power, a machine, a means of steering a course. And it's wonderful. Without it you would drift about in the air, powerless. That is what madmen do. They have deeper presentiments than the people on the pavement but they have no key and no helm to steer with and they whirl round in the abyss. But you, Sinclair, you *do* things! And how is that? You don't really know, do you? You do it with a new organ, a breath-controller. That shows you how impersonal your soul is down in its depths. It is unaware of this regulator! But it isn't new. It is a loan. It has existed for thousands of years. It is the fishes' sense of equilibrium, the air-bladder. And in point of fact there are a few strange and primeval genera of fish in which the air-bladder is a kind of lung and can function on occasion in that capacity. It closely resembles the lung you use for flying in your dreams!"

He brought along a volume of zoology for me to study and showed me the names and illustrations of these ancient fish. And with a peculiar shudder I felt conscious of a function that existed in me from earlier stages of evolution.

VI Jacob and The Angel

It is impossible to recount briefly what I learned from the eccentric musician about Abraxas. The most important thing was that it meant a step forward in the progress to self-knowledge. I was at that time an unusual youth for my eighteen years, precocious in a hundred ways, immature and helpless in a hundred others. When, on occasion, I compared myself with other people, I sometimes felt proud and conceited but often I was depressed and mortified. I had often regarded myself as a genius but no less often as half-mad. I could not successfully join in the life and pleasures of my fellows and I had frequently been consumed with self-reproach and anxiety, as if, separated from them, I was beyond hope, as if I was debarred from life.

Pistorius who himself was a grown-up eccentric taught me how to maintain my courage and self-respect. By continually finding some value in my words, dreams and fancies, and always taking and discussing them seriously, he set me an example.

"You told me that you love music because it has nothing to do with morality," he said. "That's my view too but you should beware of turning into a moralist! You shouldn't make comparisons between yourself and other people, if nature created you a bat you must not try and make yourself into an ostrich. You often look upon yourself as a special case; you propose to follow different ways from the majority. That you must unlearn. Look into the fire, gaze into the clouds and as soon as the presentiments come to you and the voices within you begin to speak, surrender to them, do not merely ask whether what you are doing suits your teacher or your father or this or that good god! That's the way to self-destruction. That would be the pedestrian way, becoming a fossil. Our god, my dear Sinclair, is called Abraxas and he is both god and devil; he contains in himself the world of light and the world of darkness. Abraxas has nothing to object to in any of your thoughts or any of your dreams. Always remember that. But once you become faultless and normal he abandons you in favour of a new vessel into which he can pour his thoughts."

Among all my dreams the dark dream of love was the most constant. I was always dreaming that I was entering our old house under the heraldic bird; I advanced to embrace my mother but she would turn out to be the large, half-male, half-maternal woman who filled me with awe and for whom I felt the most violent attraction. I could never bring myself to recount this dream to my friend. I withheld it when I had revealed everything else to him. It was my private corner, my secret, my escape.

When I was depressed, I asked Pistorius to play me old Buxtehude's Passacaglia. In the dark church in the evening I would sit lost in this strange, self-contained music, music which existed for itself and in its own right. It did me good to hear it and made me more ready to heed my own inner voice.

Sometimes we stayed for a time sitting in the church after he had finished playing the organ and watched the daylight shining feebly and losing itself in the high gothic windows.

"It seems comic to think that I was once a theological student and nearly went into the Church," said Pistorius. "But I was only committing an error in form at that time. It is my aim and vocation to be a priest. I was satisfied too early in life, however, and put myself at Jehovah's disposal before I knew Abraxas. Every religion has its own beauty. Religion is soul; it's all one whether you take part in Christian communion or make a pilgrimage to Mecca."

"You could have become a pastor, then," I said.

"No, Sinclair. I could not have been true to myself. Our religion is worn out; as if it had ceased to be a religion and had become a purely intellectual matter. I could possibly become a Roman Catholic but a Protestant priest, never! The few true believers – I know some – stick closely to the literal interpretation. I could not say to them that Christ is not a person as far as I am concerned but a hero, a myth, a vast shadow picture in which humanity sees itself projected on the walls of eternity. And the others who attend church to hear a well-turned sermon, to fulfil a duty so as to leave no stone unturned and so forth – what would I have to say to them? Convert them, do you think? But I have no desire to do that. The priest does not want to convert, all he wants is to live among believers, among his own brethren and be an instrument and expression of the feeling out of which man makes his gods."

He paused and then continued, "Our new belief for which we choose the name Abraxas is a good one, my dear friend. It is the best we have but it is still not yet weaned! It hasn't yet grown its wings. Unfortunately a solitary religion is still not the true one. It must first be enjoyed in common, must have a cult, its ecstasy, its feast and its mysteries . . ."

He was lost in thought.

"Can't one also experience mysteries alone or in a very limited circle?" I asked hesitantly.

"One can indeed," he nodded his assent. "I have long been doing so. I have practised cults for which I should have to spend years in prison if it was known. But I know it is still not yet the right one."

Suddenly he clapped me on the shoulder and I shrank back. "Young man," he said earnestly, "you have your own mysteries. I know you must have dreams which you hide from me . . . I do not want to know them but I do say this – live them, these dreams of yours; act them out, erect altars to them! It will still not be the entire solution but it *is* a way. Time alone will show whether you and I and a handful of others will renew the world. But we must renew ourselves every day; otherwise it will be hopeless. Think about it! You are eighteen years old; you don't chase after women of the streets; you must have dreams and wishes of love. Perhaps they are of the kind that frighten you. Don't be afraid! They are the best you have. Believe me, I have lost a great deal by doing violence to my dreams of love when I was your age. You shouldn't. When you know about Abraxas you cannot persist in that attitude. One should be fearless and consider nothing forbidden that our soul craves for."

Shocked, I interposed, "But you can't do everything that comes into your head. You can't do away with a person because he is hostile to you."

He stepped closer to me.

"In certain circumstances even that! In most cases, however, it is merely an error. Nor do I mean that you should simply do whatever goes through your mind. No. But you should not spoil those ideas which have their good aspect by rejecting them and moralizing about them. Instead of nailing yourself or someone else to the cross, you can drink from a chalice in solemn mood and reflect on the mystery of sacrifice. Even without all this, it is possible to treat one's actions and so-called temptations with love and respect. Then they will reveal their meaning – and they all *have* a meaning. If something that seems quite mad or sinful enters your head in the future, should you feel like murdering someone or committing some enormity, remember for a moment that it is Abraxas at work in your imagination! The person you wish to murder is never Mr. So and So. He is only a disguise. When we hate some-one we are hating something that is within ourselves, in his image. We are never stirred up by something which does not already exist within us."

Pistorius had never said anything which had a deeper

effect upon me. I could not reply. What had moved me most and in the strangest way was the similarity of this exhortation to Demian's words, which I had been carrying round with me for years. They knew nothing of each other and yet both had given me the same message.

"The things we see," said Pistorius gently, "are the things which are already in us. There is no reality beyond what we have inside us. That is why most people live such unreal lives; they take pictures outside themselves for the real ones and fail to express their own world. One can of course live contentedly enough in that situation. But once you know about the other you no longer have the choice of following the majority way. The way of the majority, Sinclair, is easy, ours is hard ... But now we must go."

Some days later after twice waiting for him in vain he came swaying along round a street-corner in the cold night wind; he was reeling along, quite drunk. I felt no wish to call after him. He went past me with shining, bewildered eyes as if he was answering some dark call from the unknown. I followed him along a street. He moved as if he was being drawn along by an invisible thread. His gait was fantastic, yet somehow free, as if he were a ghost. I returned home gloomily to my unsolved dreams.

"So that's how the world is renewed!" I thought and felt at the same instant that such a reflection was unworthy and sententious. After all, what did I know about his dreams? Perhaps the path he trod in his drunkenness was surer than the tentative one I trod.

Sometimes in the breaks between the lessons a fellow pupil to whom I had never paid any previous attention seemed anxious to talk to me. He was a small, delicate, puny individual with lank red hair and he had something odd about his mien and deportment. One evening when I went home he watched out for me in the lane to allow me to pass by; then he pursued me and posted himself in front of our door.

"Do you want something from me?" I asked.

"Only to speak to you?" he ventured shyly. "Would you mind walking a few yards with me?"

I followed him and sensed that he was very excited and full of expectancy. His hands trembled.

"Are you a spiritualist?" he asked quite suddenly.

"No, Knauer," I laughed. "Not a bit. What makes you think so?"

"But you're a theosophist?"

"Not that either."

"Oh, don't be so secretive. I am quite sure that there's something special about you. I can read it in your eyes. I am quite convinced that you are in communication with the spirit world. I am not asking out of curiosity, Sinclair, I am just a seeker and am so alone." .

"Let's hear about it," I encouraged him. "I know absolutely nothing about spirits; I live in my own dreams; that's what you have felt about me. Others live in dreams but not in their own – that's the difference."

"Yes, perhaps that's it," he murmured. "It's just a question of what kind of dreams you live in. Have you ever heard of white magic?"

I could not claim to have done so.

"It's white magic when you learn to regulate your own life. Then you can become immortal and do magic too. Haven't you ever indulged in experiments of that kind?"

At first he was reluctant to answer my inquisitive questions about these practices until I turned to move away; then he unburdened himself about the whole thing.

"For example, I myself practise that kind of magic when I want to go to sleep or concentrate. I just think of some-thing, a word or a name for instance or a geometric figure. I think about it as hard as I can and try to think it inside my brain until I feel that it has become part of it. Then I think it into my neck and so on until the idea has taken complete possession of me. Then I am so to speak 'set' and nothing else can rouse me from my peace of mind."

I had a vague idea of what he meant but I realized that he had something else on his mind for he was curiously excited and restless. I tried to be tactful with my questions and before long he asked his own.

"Are you still continent?" he asked me nervously.

"In what sense? Do you mean sexually?"

"Yes. I have been continent now for two years – since I learned by experience. Before that I was depraved, but you know that . . . Haven't you ever had a woman then?"

"No," I said. "I haven't found the right one."

"But if you did find one you considered the right one, would you go to bed with her?"

"Yes, of course. If she herself had nothing against it," I said with faint irony.

"Oh, then you are on the wrong road! You can only develop your inner resources if you stay completely continent. That's what I have done now for two whole years; two years and a little more than a month! It is so difficult! Very often I can't hold out any longer."

"Listen to me, Knauer. I don't believe continency is all that important."

"I know that's what they all say," he objected. "But I didn't expect that from you. Whoever wants to follow the spiritual path must keep absolutely pure."

"All right, do so! But I fail to understand why the person who represses his sexual desires should be considered any 'purer' than anyone else. Or can you exclude the sexual element from every thought and dream?"

He gave me a look of despair.

"No, indeed no! Heavens, and yet it seems inevitable. I have dreams at night that I could not even tell myself! Fearful dreams!"

I recalled what Pistorius had told me. But however much

I felt his words to be true, I was unable to pass them on. I found it impossible to proffer him any advice which did not emanate from my own personal experience unless I felt able to follow it myself. I was silent and felt humiliated that someone should ask advice of me when I had none to give.

"I have tried everything?" moaned Knauer. "I have done everything that can be done with cold water, snow, exercise and running but it's no use. I wake up every night from dreams which I have no right to dream. And the dreadful thing is that I gradually lose grip of the spiritual progress I have already made. I find it almost impossible to concentrate or lull myself to sleep again; I often lie awake the whole night. I can never hold out long. When I finally have to give up the struggle, yield and make myself impure again I am more despicable than all the others who haven't ever had to fight. Can you understand that?"

I nodded but did not know what to say. He was beginning to bore me and I was afraid of myself because I could not feel very deeply impressed by his despair. All I felt was 'I can't help you.'

"Then you can't tell me anything to help?" he said finally, sad and exhausted. "Absolutely nothing? But there must be a way? How do you manage?"

"I can't say, Knauer. We can't help anybody else. No one was able to help me. You must rely on yourself and then do what comes to you from within. There's no other way. If you can't find the way to yourself you won't find any spirits either, I am sure."

Disappointed and suddenly bereft of speech the little chap looked at me. Then a sudden gleam of hatred entered his eye and he grimaced and shrieked, "You're a fine saint! You've got your secret vice too! You play the wise man and secretly you cling to the same dirt as I do and everybody else! You're a swine like me. We're all of us swine!"

I went off and left him standing there. He took two or

three steps after me, hesitated, turned round and ran off. I felt ill, with mixed feelings of disgust and sympathy and I was unable to rid myself of this nausea until I had arranged my few pictures round me in my little room and given myself up to my private dreams with intense fervour. Then my dream returned at once – our gateway and the coat-of-arms, my mother and the strange woman whose features I saw with such a preternatural clarity that I was able to draw her portrait from memory the same evening.

When this drawing was completed a few days later and had been painted in almost unconsciously during the odd ten minutes in between times, I hung it on my wall the same evening, pushed the study lamp in front of it and stood before it as before a spirit with whom I had to fight it out. The face was similar to the previous one, similar to my friend Demian and in some ways resembled me. One eye was perceptibly higher than the other and her glance looked over and beyond me with a fateful stare.

I stood before her and the nervous strain made my blood run cold. I questioned the picture, accused it, caressed it, prayed to it, called it mother, sweetheart, whore and strumpet, I called it Abraxas. Meantime sayings of Pistorius – or were they Demian's – came into my head; I could not recall when they had been uttered but I imagined I could hear them again. They were remarks about Jacob wrestling with the angel of God and his 'I will not let thee go except thou bless me.'

The painted face in the lamp-light changed at every utterance I made – light and shining, dark and sinister, livid lids closed over glazed eyes which opened again and darted loving glances – it was woman, man, girl, small child, animal, then it melted away to a small speck, grew large and clear again. At length I yielded to the strong impulse to shut my eyes and now saw the image within myself, more vivid and powerful than ever. I wanted to prostrate myself before it but it was so much part of me that I was unable to leave it – as if it had just turned into me myself.

Then I heard a dark, thunderous roar as though from a spring storm and I trembled in an indescribably novel feeling of fear and misadventure. Stars flashed before my eyes and were extinguished. Memories which went back to forgotten infancy, nay pre-existence, and the first stages of being, hurried past me. But the memories which seemed to rehearse my whole life in its deepest intimacy did not stop with the past and present, they went further, mirrored the future, tore me away from the present into new forms of life whose images were fantastically clear and dazzling though I was unable to recapture a single one later.

In the night I awoke out of my profound sleep. I was still dressed and lay diagonally across the bed. I switched on the light, felt I must remember something important but could recall nothing of the hours that had passed. I lit the lamp. The memory gradually returned. I looked for the picture; it no longer hung on the wall, it was not on the table either. Then I had a vague feeling that I had burned it. Or had I merely dreamed that I had burnt it in my hands and eaten the ashes?

A great restlessness seized hold of me; I put on my hat; strode out through the house and along the lane as if I were being driven by some outward force; ran on and on through streets and across squares as though blown by gusts of wind; listened by the dark church of my friend, blindly seeking for something without knowing what it was. I passed through a suburb where there were brothels that had a light here and there in the windows. Farther out still stood some new buildings and piles of bricks partially covered with grey-coloured snow. As I wandered like a somnambulist under the influence of this strange impulse I noticed the new building of my home town; it was there that my tormentor Kromer had taken me for our first financial settlement. A similar building lay before me in the grey night, yawned at me with its gaping door. It drew me in; I had no choice and I advanced, stumbling over heaps of sand and rubbish; the urge was irresistible; I had to enter. I staggered into the dreary room over planks and broken bricks; it smelt depressingly of damp cold and stones. There was a heap of sand, a light stain of grey – all the rest was dark.

Then a voice cried out in terror, "For God's sake, Sinclair, where have you come from?"

And a figure rose out of the darkness, a small, lean fellow like a ghost. My hair stood on end, I recognized my schoolmate Knauer.

"How do you come to be here?" he asked, almost mad with emotion, "How did you manage to find me?"

I did not understand what he meant.

"I wasn't searching for you," I said, dazed, and every word I said cost me an effort and was forced wearily through my heavy, as it were frozen, lips.

He stared at me.

"Not searching?"

"No. I felt drawn here. Did you call me? You must have called me. What are you doing here then? It's night."

He clasped me tightly in his thin arms.

"Yes, night. It will soon be morning. Oh, Sinclair, how wonderful that you haven't forgotten me! Can you forgive me then?"

"What for?"

"Oh dear, I was so odious!"

Only at this point did I recall our conversation. Had it occurred four or five days ago? It seemed a lifetime since then. But now suddenly it all became clear. Not only what had happened between us but why I had come hither and what Knauer had wanted to do out there.

"You intended to take your life, then, Knauer?"

He shivered with cold and fear.

"Yes, I intended to. I don't know whether I could have

done. I intended to wait until it was morning."

I drew him out into the open air. The first horizontal streaks of dawn glimmered unbelievably cold and joyless in the grey air.

I led the boy for a while by the arm. I heard myself say, "Now go home and don't say a word to anyone! You've been treading the wrong path, the false path! We are not the swine you spoke of. We are human beings. We make gods and do battle with them and they bless us."

We walked on in silence and parted company. When I reached home it was daylight.

The best things I gained from my remaining days in St. —— were the hours I spent listening to Pistorius at the organ or in front of the fire. We were studying a Greek text together about Abraxas and he read out extracts from a translation from the *Vedas* and taught me how to speak the sacred 'Om.' But it was not these bits of occult learning that provided my inner sustenance; rather the contrary. What encouraged me was the progress within myself, my increasing faith in my own dreams, thoughts and presentiments and my increasing knowledge of the power I possessed within me.

I had a complete understanding with Pistorius. I only needed to think hard of him and could be sure that he – or a message from him – would come. I could ask him anything, as I would Demian, without his having to be present in person; all I had to do was to imagine him there and frame my questions in the form of intensive thoughts. Then all the spiritual effort that I had expended in the question came back to me with like force. Only, it was not the person of Pistorius, nor that of Demian that I conjured up but the painted picture, the half male, half female fantasy of my daimon which I had to evoke. This being was now no longer confined to my dreams, no longer merely depicted on paper; it was in me like a wish-fulfilment and enhanced version of myself. The relationship which the would-be suicide, Knauer, had now established with me was peculiar, sometimes laughable. Ever since the night during which I had been 'sent to him' he clung to me like a faithful servant or dog, made every effort to link his life with mine and followed me around blindly. He came to me with the most astonishing questions and requests, wanted to see spirits, learn the *cabbala* and refused to believe me when I assured him that I did not understand all these mysteries. He thought nothing was beyond my powers. But the strange thing was that he often approached me with his wonderful and stupid questions just at a moment when I was faced with some problem to which his moody ideas or requests often provided the clue and set me on the road towards a solution. He was often a bore and I would dismiss him peremptorily but I still had the feeling that he too was sent to me, that from him too came back whatever I gave him – in double measure, he too was a leader for me or at any rate represented a way to follow. The mad books and writings which he brought to me and in which he sought his salvation taught me more than I could comprehend at the time.

Later on Knauer slipped unnoticed out of my life. A formal parting was not necessary. It was just the opposite with Pistorius. Towards the conclusion of my schooldays in St. —— I still had a strange experience to share with him.

Even the most harmless of human beings cannot altogether escape coming into conflict with the praiseworthy virtues of piety and gratitude on one or two occasions in their lives. Sooner or later everyone must take the step that separates him from his father and teachers; everyone must experience something of the hardness of solitude even if most human beings cannot take much of it and soon crawl back. I myself did not make a sudden or violent break from my parents and their world, my childhood 'world of light,' but I slowly, almost imperceptibly, drew further and further away from them. I was sorry and suffered many galling hours during my visits home but I was not fundamentally affected; it was bearable.

But where we have given of our love and respect not from habit but of our own free will, where we have been children and friends from our inmost heart, it is a bitter and terrible moment when we suddenly recognize that our natural tendency is bound to lead us away from the people we love. Then every thought which alienates the friend and teacher turns back into our own heart with poisoned barbs; then every defensive blow comes back at one's own face, then the words 'infidelity' and 'ingratitude' surge up like shameful cries and branding irons in the mind of the person who has preciously prided himself on his sound moral behaviour, and the frightened heart flees timidly back to the charmed valleys of childish virtues; unable to believe that this break too must be made, this bond also be severed.

As time went on my unquestioning acknowledgment of my friend Pistorius as a leader had been modified. My friendship with him, his counsel, his proximity, the comfort he had brought, had been the most vital experiences of those months of my adolescence. God had spoken to me through him. From his lips my dreams had been returned to me, explained and interpreted. He had restored my faith in myself. And now, alas, I was becoming conscious of a gradually increasing opposition to him within me. I found too much didacticism in his words; I felt that he only fully understood one part of me.

No quarrel or scene occurred between us, no break, not even an agreement to differ. I merely uttered one single, harmless phrase – but it was in that precise moment that an illusion was shattered and fell between us like so many coloured fragments.

A vague presentiment of such a happening had already depressed me for some time and it took a definite shape one Sunday in his old study. We were lying on the floor by the fire and he was talking about the mysteries and forms of religion which he was studying and turning over in his mind and the future potentialities of which preoccupied him. All this seemed to me more an object of curiosity and interest than a really vital matter; it had a pedagogic ring about it; it sounded like tedious research among the fragments of ancient worlds. And all at once I felt a repugnance against the whole business, this cult of mythologies, this mosaic game he was playing with fragments of traditional religious beliefs.

"Pistorius," I said suddenly in a fit of malice which both surprised and frightened me. "You ought to tell me a dream – a real dream – one that you have dreamed during the night. What you are telling me is all so damned antiquarian!"

He had never heard me speak like that before and I immediately realized with a mixture of shame and horror that the arrow which I had fired at him and with which I had pierced his heart, had come from his own armoury – and that I was now returning to him with sharpened barbs the self-reproaches which I had sometimes heard him utter in his ironical way.

He reacted instantaneously and fell silent at once. I glanced at him with dread in my heart and saw that he had gone terribly pale.

After a long, uneasy pause, he threw some fresh logs on the fire and said in a quiet voice, "You are quite right, Sinclair. You're a clever fellow and I will spare you the 'antiquarian' stuff." Although he spoke calmly he was obviously hurt. What had I done?

I was very near tears; I wanted to speak a message of encouragement, implore his forgiveness, assure him of my affection, my deep gratitude. Words of comfort rose to my lips but I could not utter them. I continued to lie there, gazing into the fire and kept silent. He kept silent too and so we lay and the fire dwindled and with every dying flame I felt something beautiful and profound that could never return glow and disappear.

"I am afraid you misunderstand me," I said at length dejectedly in a dry, hoarse voice. These stupid and senseless words fell mechanically from my lips as if I was reading from a magazine serial.

"I understand you perfectly well," said Pistorius gently. "You are right," He paused. Then he continued slowly, "that is as far as one man can be right against anyone else."

A voice inside me said, 'No, no, I am wrong,' but I could not say it aloud. I knew that with my brief words I had put my finger on his fundamental weakness, his affliction and wound. I had probed the place where he was unsure of himself. His ideal was 'antiquarian' – he was a seeker in the past, a romantic. And suddenly I realized very forcibly that what Pistorius had been and had given to me was precisely what he could never be and give to himself. He had shown me a way which even he, the leader, must by-pass and abandon.

God knows how the words had sprung to my lips! I had not intended them in any derogatory sense, had not anticipated their disastrous effect. I had said something of whose significance I myself was not aware at the moment of speaking; I had yielded to a vague, somewhat petty and mischievous impulse and it had been charged with fate. I had committed a trivial and heedless gaucherie which he regarded as a judgment on him.

How much I wished at that time that he would fly into a temper; defend himself and storm about me. But he did nothing of the kind. I had to do all that for him inside myself. He would have forced a smile if he could have managed it. The fact that he found it impossible was the surest proof of the extent of the injury I had done him.

Meantime, by accepting this blow so quietly from an

impudent and ungrateful pupil, by remaining silent and taking the rebuff, by acknowledging what I had said as his fate, he made me odious in my own eyes and my indiscretion a hundred times worse. When I had hit out I thought I was aiming my blow at a tough, well-armed man but now it turned out to be a quiet, suffering defenceless creature who was surrendering without a protest.

We stayed for a long time in front of the glimmering fire, and every flowing shape, every writhing twig evoked the rich and pleasurable hours of the past and brought home more and more my indebtedness to Pistorius. Finally I could bear it no longer. I rose to my feet and went. For long enough I stood at his door; for long enough I stood on the dark stairs, for long enough outside, waiting by the door in case he should follow me. Then I continued my way and tramped along for hours and hours through the town and suburbs, park and woods until evening. Then for the first time, I was conscious of the mark of Cain on my forehead. It was only gradually that I became aware of this. My thoughts were all aimed in one direction – accusing myself and defending Pistorius. Yet it ended the other way round, for although I was prepared to regret and take back my hasty word I felt that what I had said was true. Now for the first time I understood Pistorius and was able to reconstruct in my mind the whole dream that he had set himself to fulfil. He had wanted to be a priest, to announce the new religion, provide new forms for the movement, serve it with love and devotion and create a series of new symbols. But it was beyond his power to do so; this could never be his function. He lingered too much in the past, his knowledge of ancient days was too precise; he knew far too much about Egypt, India, Mithras and Abraxas. His love was bound up with symbols that the world had already seen and in his heart of hearts he realized that the New must be really new and different and must spring up from new soil and not be created from museums and libraries. Perhaps his function was to help to lead men to themselves – as he had done in my case – not to provide them with the yet unspoken message and their new gods.

And at this point I felt the truth burning within me like a sharp flame, that there was some role for everybody but it was not one which he himself could choose, re-cast and regulate to his own liking. One had no right to want new gods, no right at all to want to give the world anything of that sort! There was but one duty for a grown man; it was to seek the way to himself, to become resolute within, to grope his way forward wherever that might lead him. The discovery shook me profoundly; it was the fruit of this experience. I had often toyed with pictures of the future, dreamed of roles which might be assigned to me – as a poet, maybe, or prophet or painter or kindred vocation. All that was futile. I was not there to write poetry, to preach or paint; neither I nor any other man was there for that purpose. They were only incidental things. There was only one true vocation for everybody – to find the way to himself. He might end as poet, lunatic, prophet or criminal – that was not his affair; ultimately it was of no account. *His* affair was to discover his own destiny, not something of his own choosing, and live it out wholly and resolutely within himself. Anything else was merely a half life, an attempt at evasion, an escape into the ideals of the masses, complacency and fear of his inner soul. The new picture rose before me, sacred and awe-inspiring, a hundred times glimpsed, possibly often expressed and now experienced for the first time. I was an experiment on the part of nature, a 'throw' into the unknown, perhaps for some new purpose, perhaps for nothing and my only vocation was to allow this 'throw' to work itself out in my innermost being, feel its will within me and make it wholly mine. That or nothing!

I had already tasted much loneliness. Now I felt that

there was a deeper loneliness, a loneliness that was inescapable.

I made no attempt at a reconciliation with Pistorius. We remained friends but the relationship had changed. On one occasion only did we refer to the conversation. He said "You know that I wished to become a priest. Above all I wanted to be the priest of the new religion of which you and I have so many presentiments. That rôle can never be mine. I know it and I have known it for a long time without wholly admitting it to myself. I now intend to undertake another kind of priestly service – perhaps on the organ, perhaps some other way. But I must always have things around me that I find beautiful and sacred – organ music and mystery, symbol and myth. I need those and cannot renounce them. That is my weakness. For often enough, Sinclair, I know that I ought not to have desires of this kind, that they are luxury and weakness. It would be larger-minded and juster if I put myself quite unreservedly at the disposal of fate. But that I cannot do; it is the only thing I cannot do. But perhaps you can. It is difficult; it is the only really difficult thing there is. I have often dreamed of doing so; but I cannot; I am afraid. I am not capable of standing so naked and alone; I am a poor weak dog who needs warmth and food and likes the comfort of having his fellow creatures near him. The man who really wants nothing beyond his destiny no longer has his neighbours beside him; he stands quite alone and has nothing but the cold world around him. Jesus in the Garden of Gethsemane. There have been martyrs who let themselves be nailed to the cross without a murmur, but even these were not heroes, were not 'freed' for even they wanted something that was homely and familiar to them – they had models, they had ideals. But the man who follows his destiny is allowed neither models nor ideals; nothing cherished or comforting! And yet this is the path one must follow. People like you and me are truly lonely but we still have each other; we have the secret satisfaction of being different, of putting up resistance, of desiring the unusual. But one must cast aside that too if one wishes to go the whole way. One may not be revolutionary, an example or a martyr either. It is beyond imagining."

Yes, it was beyond imagining, but it could be dreamed of, anticipated, felt. Sometimes I had a slight experience of it when I found a whole quiet hour to myself. At such times I would look into myself and see the image of my destiny in the staring eyes. They could be full of wisdom, full of madness; they could glow with love or dire evil – it was all the same. You could not choose, you ought not to want anything; only *yourself*, your own fate. Pistorius had served me as a guide on part of my journey.

In those days I ran around like a blind man. Storms raged inside me; every step was danger. I saw nothing in front of me except the abysmal darkness into which all former paths ended and vanished. And within myself I saw the image of the leader who resembled Demian and in whose eyes my fate could be read.

I wrote on a piece of paper: "A leader has abandoned me. I am standing in utter darkness. I cannot take another step alone. Help me!"

I wanted to send a message to Demian. Yet I forebore; each time the impulse came, it seemed so feeble and senseless. But I knew my little prayer by heart and often uttered it silently. It accompanied me every hour. I began to have some inkling of what prayer meant.

My schooldays were over. I was to make a holiday tour which my father had planned. Then I was to proceed to the university, but I did not know what subject I was expected to read. I was allowed to do philosophy for a term. Any other subject would have done as well.

VII Eva

One time during the holidays I visited the house where, years before, Demian had lived with his mother. An old woman was strolling in the garden, I spoke to her and learned that the house belonged to her. I inquired after the Demian family. She remembered them very well, but she did not know where they lived at present. Sensing my interest in them, she took me into the house, looked out a leather album and showed me a photograph of Demian's mother. I could hardly remember her but now that I had the small photograph before me my heart stood still. It was the picture of my dreams. There she was, the tall, almost masculine figure, looking like her son, but with maternal traits, traits of severity and deep passion, beautiful and alluring, beautiful and unapproachable, daimon and mother, fate and lover. There was no mistaking her!

The discovery that my dream image existed on this earth affected me like some fantastic miracle! So there was a woman who looked like that, who bore the features of my destiny! Where was she? Where? And she was Demian's mother!

Shortly after this I embarked on my journey. A strange journey! I travelled restlessly from place to place, following every impulse, always searching for this woman. There were days when everyone I met reminded me of her, echoed her, resembled her, enticed me along the alleys in strange cities, railway stations, trains, like a confused dream. There were other days when I saw how futile my search was. Then I would sit idly somewhere in a park, a hotel garden, a waiting-room, look into myself and endeavour to bring life back to the image within me. But it had now become shy and evanescent. I was unable to sleep. I had to be satisfied with cat-naps on railway journeys through unknown landscapes. Once a woman in Zurich followed me. She was a pretty, somewhat impudent creature. I hardly looked at her, but continued on my way as if she were made of air. I would have rather died then and there than pay attention to any other woman even for an hour.

I felt that my fate was drawing me on. I felt that the moment of fulfilment was approaching and I was mad with impatience at not being able to do anything about it. Once in a station – I think it was Innsbruck – I caught sight of a woman who reminded me of Eva. She was seated by the window in a train that was just starting, and I was miserable for days. And suddenly the form reappeared in a dream one night; I woke up feeling humiliated and dejected by the futility of my hunt and made my way back home.

A few weeks later I was enrolled as a member of the university of H——. I found everything disappointing. The course of lectures on the history of philosophy which I attended was as uninspired and stereotyped as the activities of the undergraduates. They were all so much to pattern; everybody behaved in an identical way and the animated gaiety on their boyish faces looked empty and artificial. But I was free! I had the whole day to myself, I lived in peace and comfort in a tumble-down house just outside the town and I had a few volumes of Nietzsche on my table. I lived with him, felt the loneliness of his soul, shared his prescience of the fate that drove him unceasingly on, suffered with him and rejoiced that there had been one man who had relentlessly followed his destiny.

Late one evening I was strolling through the town. An autumn wind was blowing and I could hear members of student clubs singing in the taverns. Clouds of tobacco smoke came from the opened windows with a profusion of songs, loud, solemn yet uninspired and uniformly dead.

I stood at the street corner listening as this punctually rehearsed gaiety of youth rang out in the night from the two inns. Community spirit everywhere, sitting about together everywhere, everywhere escape from fate and flight to cosy firesides!

Two men were walking slowly behind me. I caught a snatch of their conversation.

"Isn't it just like the young men's house in a negro village?" said one. "Everything's the same down to the tattooing which is now in fashion. Look, there you have young Europe."

The voice sounded amazingly familiar – I'd heard it before. I followed the two of them along the dark lane; one was Japanese, small and elegant; I could see his smiling yellow face gleaming under a street-lamp.

The other was now speaking again.

"I don't suppose it is any better with you in Japan. The people who don't make a bee-line for the fireside are rare the whole world over. There are some here too."

I felt a mixture of joy and alarm as each word he said went through me. I knew the speaker. It was Demian.

I followed him and the Japanese through the gusty night, along the dark lanes, listened to their conversation and Demian's voice was as music in my ear. It had the familiar ring, the familiar assurance and calm and all its old power over me. Everything was set to rights again. I had found him.

When they arrived at the end of a street in the suburbs the Japanese took his leave and opened the door of a house. Demian retraced his steps; I had stood still, waiting for him in the middle of the street. My heart beat fast as I saw him coming towards me, with his springy tread and upright carriage. He was wearing a fawn mackintosh and a thin walking stick dangled from his arm. He came on without any change in his uniform pace until he had practically reached me, then he removed his hat and I obtained a clearer view of the familiar intelligent face with the determined mouth and the peculiar radiance of his broad forehead.

"Demian!" I called out.

He stretched his hand out towards me.

"So it's you, Sinclair! I have been expecting you."

"Did you know I was here then?"

"Not exactly, but I certainly hoped you were. I didn't see you until tonight; you've been on our tracks the whole time."

"Did you recognize me straight away then?"

"Of course. You have changed, naturally. But you still have the mark on you."

"The 'mark'? What sort of mark?"

"In the old days we called it 'the mark of Cain' if you still remember. It's our sign. You have always had it – that's how I became your friend. But it's more evident now."

"I wasn't aware of that. But on second thoughts, yes, I was. Once I painted a picture of you, Demian, and I was astonished to find that it resembled me. Was that the 'mark'?"

"Yes, that was it. Good! now you've understood! My mother will be pleased too."

This frightened me.

"Your mother? Is she here? But she doesn't know me."

"She knows about you. She will recognize you without my having to tell her who you are . . . You've kept us without news of you for a long time."

"I often wanted to write but I couldn't. For some time now I have felt in my bones that I must soon find you. I've been waiting for that every day."

He thrust his arm under mine and walked along with me. An atmosphere of calm surrounded him which infected me.

We were soon chatting as we used to in the old days.

Our thoughts went back to our time at school, the confirmation classes, also the more unfortunate period in the holidays – only now our conversation was confined to our earliest and closest relationship and the Franz Kromer business was not mentioned.

Without noticing it we had got on to strange and mysterious topics. We talked – like an echo of Demian's exchanges of views with his Japanese friend – of student life and other things that seemed a far cry from that and yet there was a fundamental and inner unity of idea behind everything Demian said.

He spoke of the spirit of Europe and the signs of the times. On all sides, he said, we were seeing the reign of cooperation and the herd instinct, love and freedom nowhere. All this communal spirit from student club and glee-club to the same spirit in government was an inevitable development, it was community life based on anxiety, fear and opportunism; within it was an outworn and indolent way of life approaching its collapse.

"Communal spirit," said Demian, "is a fine thing. But what we now see flourishing everywhere is not really that. The real spirit will rise up, new, from the separate contribution of each individual and for a time it will transform the world. The only manifestation of communal spirit to be seen at present is the herd-instinct at work. Human beings fly into each other's arms because they are afraid of each other – the masters afraid for themselves. They are a community composed entirely for themselves! And why are they afraid? Man is only afraid when he is not attuned to himself. They are afraid because they have never made themselves known to themselves. They are a community composed entirely of men who are afraid of the unknown element within themselves! They are all conscious of the fact that the laws of life they have inherited are no longer valid, that they are living according to archaic tablets of the law that neither their religion nor customs are adapted to our present-day needs. For a hundred years or so Europe has done nothing but study and build factories! They know exactly how many grams of explosive are needed to kill a man but they do not know how to pray to God, they do not even know how to remain happy and contented for one single hour. Just look at a students' club, like this. Or indeed any place of amusement where rich people congregate. Hopeless! My dear Sinclair, nothing encouraging can emerge from that kind of thing. These men who come together in this nervous fashion are riddled with fear and evil: none of them trust each other. They cling to ideals which no longer exist, and stone anyone who sets up a new one. I have a presentiment that great divisions lie ahead. They will come, believe me! and come soon! Naturally they will not 'improve' the world. Whether the workers murder the manufacturers or the Russians and Germans shoot each other, it will merely be a change of ownership. But it won't have been in vain. It will show up the bankruptcy of the present-day ideal; there will be a sweeping away of stone-age gods. This world as it is now constituted, will perish, will be destroyed, it's happening before our eyes."

"And what will become of us in the meantime?" I asked.

"Us? Perhaps we will be destroyed with it. But even that does not absolve us from responsibility. Around whatever remains of us, or around those of us who survive the catastrophe, will gather the spirit of the future. The will of humanity which this Europe of ours with its science and industry fairs has shouted down for a time will be revealed. It will then become clear that the will of humanity is never and nowhere to be identified with that of our present communities, states and nations, clubs and churches. No; what nature wants of man is written in a few individuals, in you, in me. It was written in Christ, it was written in Nietzsche. Only for these important currents alone – which can of course assume a different form every day – will there be a place when the communities of today collapse."

It was late when we stopped in front of a garden by the river.

"This is where we live," said Demian. "Come and visit us soon! We want to see you very much."

Full of elation I retraced my long way back through the now chilly night air. Here and there noisy students were reeling home through the town. I had often marked the contrast between their comic kind of merriment and my solitary life, sometimes with scorn, sometimes with a feeling of deprivation. But never until today had I realized with calm and quiet confidence how little it mattered to me and how remote and dead all that world now was for me. I called to mind the civil servants in my own town, worthy old gentlemen who clung to the memories of their drunken university days as if they were memories of a blessed paradise, and upon the vanished 'freedom' of their student years built a cult similar to that which poets or other 'Romantics' formerly devoted to childhood. Was it everywhere alike? It was always somewhere in the past that they looked for 'freedom' and 'happiness' out of sheer dread lest they should be reminded of their own responsibilities and their own future course. They drank and made merry for a few years; then they crawled into their shells and became serious-minded men in the service of the state. Yes, it was indolence, the spirit of indolence among us, and this student stupidity at least was not so stupid and evil as countless other stupidities.

By the time I had arrived at my distant home and was preparing for bed, all these thoughts had vanished and the whole of my mind was focused expectantly on the great hope which the day had brought me. I was to be allowed to see Demian's mother as soon as I wished, tomorrow! The students could hold their drunken celebrations, tattoo their faces, the world could be indolent and wait for its destruction for all I cared! I was only waiting for one thing – for my fate to approach me in a new guise.

I slept hard until late in the morning. The new day dawned like a solemn feast-day of the kind I had not experienced since boyhood. I was full of great restlessness but devoid of any sort of fear. I felt that an important day had dawned for me, I saw and experienced a changed world around me, expectant, meaningful and solemn, even the gentle autumn rain had its beauty and a calm festive air full of happy, sacred music. For the first time the outer world was perfectly attuned to the world within me as when it is a special day for the heart and one feels that it is blessed to be alive. No house, no shop-window, no face disturbed me in the street; everything was as it should be, without any of the flat and humdrum look of the everyday, ready and expectant to face its destiny with reverence. It was how the world had appeared to me, a small boy on the mornings of the big feast-days, Christmas and Easter. I had forgotten that the world could still be so lovely. I had grown accustomed to my inner life, resigned to the fact that I had lost my feeling for the outside world and that the loss of its bright colours was an inseparable part of the loss of childhood and that one must to some extent pay for the freedom and maturity of the soul with the renunciation of those pure gleams of light. But now, entranced, I saw that all this had only been clouded over and that it was still possible as a 'liberated' person and renouncer of childhood happiness to see the world shine and savour the delicious thrill of the child's vision.

A moment came when I found my way back to the garden on the outskirts of the town where I had taken my leave of Max Demian that night. Hidden behind high walls and mist-grey trees stood a little house, bright and homely. Tall plants grew behind a high glass wall; behind glistening windows were dark walls with pictures and bookshelves. The front door led straight into a small heated hall, and a silent dark-skinned old maid servant, with a white apron, showed me in and took my coat.

She left me alone in the hall. I looked around me and was immediately swept into the middle of my dream, for high up on the dark-panelled wall, above a door, hung a familiar picture in a black frame. It was my bird with the golden-yellow sparrow-hawk's head, struggling out of its terrestrial shell. Taken aback, I stood there motionless – in my heart were mixed feelings of joy and pain as if that moment everything I had done and experienced before was coming back to me in the form of a reply and a fulfilment. I saw a host of pictures flashing past my mind's eye – the house at home with the old coat-of-arms above the door arch, the boy Demian sketching the carving, myself as a boy, terribly involved in the evil spell of my enemy Kromer, myself in adolescence, in my schoolroom by the table quietly painting the bird of my desire, my soul lost in the intricacy of its own threads – and everything, everything up to the present moment found a new echo in me, was corroborated, answered, approved.

With eyes moistened with tears I gazed at my painting, absorbed in my reflections. Then my glance dropped. Under the picture of the bird in the opened door stood a tall woman in a dark dress. It was she.

I was unable to utter a word. From a face that resembled her son's, timeless and ageless and full of inward strength, the beautiful, dignified woman gave me a friendly smile. Her gaze was fulfilment, her greeting a homecoming.

Silently I stretched out my hands towards her. She took them both in her warm, firm hands.

"You are Sinclair. I recognized you at once. Welcome!"

Her voice was deep and warm. I drank it up like sweet wine. And now I looked up and into her quiet face, the black unfathomable eyes, at her fresh, ripe lips, the open, queenly brow that bore the 'sign.'

"How glad I am!" I said and kissed her hands. "I

believe I have been on my way here the whole of my life – and now I have reached home at last."

She gave a motherly smile.

"One never reaches home," she said amiably. "But wherever friendly paths intersect the whole world looks like home for a time."

She was expressing what I had felt on my way to her. Her voice and even her words were like her son's yet at the same time quite different. Everything about her was riper, warmer, more assured. But just as Max in the old days had never given the impression of being a boy, his mother did not look like the mother of a grown-up son, so young and charming was the aura that surrounded her face and her hair, so firm and smooth her fair skin, so fresh her lips. More regal even than in my dreams she stood before me and this closeness was bliss, her gaze fulfilment.

This then was the new form in which my fate was to reveal itself, no longer stern, no longer setting me apart but fresh and cheerful! I made no resolutions, took no vows – I had attained my goal, the high point from which the continuing path was revealed distant and attractive, climbing to the Promised Land, shaded by tree-tops of approaching happiness, cooled by near-by gardens of every joy. Whatever might happen to me, I was blessed in my knowledge that this woman was in the world, that I could drink in her voice and breathe her presence. If she could only become a mother to me, a lover, a goddess – if she could just be here! if only my path could be close to hers!

She pointed up to my sparrow-hawk picture.

"You never gave Max more pleasure than with this picture," she said reflectively. "And me too. We have been expecting you – when the painting came we knew that you were on your way to us. When you were a small boy, Sinclair, my son came back home from school one day and said, 'There's a boy there who has the "mark" on his forehead; I must have him for my friend.' It was you.

132

You've not had an easy time but we had confidence in you. You came across Max again when you were at home on holiday. You were about sixteen years old. Max told me about it . . ."

I interrupted, "He told you that! That was the most miserable period in my life!"

"Yes, Max said to me, 'Sinclair has his worst time coming now. He is making another attempt to take refuge among the others. He has even become a pub-crawler; but he won't be successful. His "mark" is momentarily obscured but it sears him secretly underneath.' Isn't that true?"

"Oh yes, exactly like that. Then I discovered Beatrice. and then at last, a guide came to me. He was called Pistorius. Only then did it become clear why my boyhood had been so closely bound up with Demian and why I could not escape from him. Dear Eva, dear mother, I often thought I should have to take my own life. Is the way as difficult as this for everybody?"

She caressed my hair with her hand. It felt as light as a breeze.

"It is always difficult to be born. You know the bird did not find it easy to struggle out of the egg. Think back and ask yourself, was the way so hard then? Wasn't it beautiful too? Could you have wished a more beautiful or easier path?"

I shook my head.

"It was hard," I said as if I were asleep, "it was hard until the dream came."

She nodded and looked right into me.

"Yes, you must find your dream, then the way becomes easy. But no dream lasts, each dream releases a new one and you should not wish to cling fast to any particular one."

I was profoundly shaken. Was that a warning note already? Was that a defensive move already? But it was all one; I was prepared to allow myself to be guided by her and not inquire about the goal.

"I do not know," I said, "how long my dream will last. I wish it could be eternal. My fate has received me under the picture of the bird like a mother, and like a lover. I belong to it and nothing else."

"While the dream is your fate, and as long as you remain faithful to it," she confirmed in serious tones.

I was overcome by a sudden sadness and a longing to die in that enchanted hour. I felt my tears – what an infinity of time since I had last wept – well unceasingly in my eyes and I could not restrain them. I turned violently on my heel, walked to the window and gazed into the distance beyond the plant-pots with tear-blinded eyes.

I heard her voice behind me; it was calm and yet as brimming with tenderness as a wine-filled beaker.

"Sinclair, you are a child! Your 'fate' loves you indeed. One day it will be wholly yours as you dream it will be if you remain constant to it."

I had regained my self-control and I turned my face towards her again. She gave me her hand.

"I have a few friends," she said smiling, "just a handful of very close friends who call me 'Frau Eva.' You shall be one of them if you wish."

She led me to the door, opened it and indicated the garden. "You will find Max out there."

I stood dazed and shaken under the tall trees; I did not know whether I was more awake or more in a dream than ever. The rain dripped gently from the branches. Slowly I walked out into the garden which bordered the river. Finally I found Demian, He was standing in an open summer-house, stripped to the waist and was doing some boxing practice with a suspended sandbag.

I stopped, amazed. Demian looked strikingly handsome with his broad chest and firm, manly head; the raised arms with taut muscles were large and powerful, the movements came from the hips, shoulders and arms like gushing springs.

"Demian?" I called. "What are you doing here?"

He gave a cheerful laugh.

"Practising. I've promised the little Jap a boxing match; he's as agile as a kitten, and just as full of tricks, of course. But he won't pull it off with me. It is a slight act of abasement that I owe him."

He drew on his shirt and jacket.

"You've just been with mother, I suppose?" he asked.

"Yes, Demian, and what a wonderful mother you have! Frau Eva! The name suits her admirably; she's like a universal mother."

He looked into my face thoughtfully for a moment.

"So you know her name already? You may well be proud, my lad. You're the first person she's told it to in the first hour of meeting."

From this day on I went in and out of their house like a son and brother – and a lover too. When I closed the door behind me, or rather as soon as I saw the tall trees in the garden rise up, I felt rich and happy. Outside was 'reality,' outside were streets and houses, human beings, institutions, libraries and classrooms – but here was love and soul, this was the home of dream and legend. And yet we lived in no way cut off from the outside world; we often lived in the midst of it in our thoughts and discussions but on different ground. We were not divided off from the majority of men by boundaries but by another kind of vision. It was our function to represent an island in the world, a kind of prototype perhaps, to proclaim in our lives new potentialities by our way of living. I, who had been a solitary so long, learned about the companionship which is possible between human beings who have tasted utter and complete loneliness. I no longer hankered after the tables of the fortunate nor the feasts of the blessed. I was no longer affected by envy or nostalgia when I watched the community life of others. And slowly I was initiated into the secret of those who bear the 'sign' on their brow.

We who bore the 'sign' might rightly be considered odd by the world, even mad and dangerous. We were 'awake' or 'wakening' and our striving was directed at an ever-increasing wakefulness, whereas the striving and quest for happiness of the rest was aimed at identifying their thoughts, ideals, duties, their lives and fortunes more and more closely with that of the herd. That too was striving, that too was power and greatness. But whereas we, in our conception, represented the will of nature to renew itself, to individualize and march forward, the others lived in the desire for the perpetuation of things as they are. For them humanity – which they loved as we did – was something complete that must be maintained and protected. For us humanity was a distant goal towards which we were marching, whose image no one yet knew, whose laws were nowhere written down.

Apart from Frau Eva, Max and myself many seekers of a very varied kind were closely or in a more general way attached to our circle. Many of them followed particular paths, had chosen special aims, put their faith in specific ideas and duties. They included astrologers, cabbalists and a disciple of Count Tolstoy and all manner of sensitive, shy, vulnerable men, members of new sects, devotees of Indian practices, vegetarians and so forth. With all these we had no common spiritual bond save the respect which each of us accorded the secret ideal of the other. Those who were concerned with man's pursuit of gods and new ideals in the past were closer to us. Their preoccupations often reminded me of those of Pistorius. They brought books with them, translated texts of ancient tongues to us, showed us illustrations of ancient symbols and rites, and taught us to see how the whole possession of humanity so far consisted of ideals that emanated from the unconscious soul, dreams in which humanity groped after the vague notions they had of their future potentialities. Thus we made our way through the wonderful, thousand-headed throng of the gods of the ancient world up to the dawn of the Christian conversion. We learned about the creeds of solitary saints and the changes of religion among different races. And from everything we collected in this way we gained a critical understanding of our time and contemporary Europe which with prodigious efforts had created new weapons for mankind but had ended by falling into a deep and final desolation of the spirit. For it had conquered the whole world only to lose its own soul in the process.

The circle also included believers and adherents of particular hopes and faiths. There were Buddhists who were eager to convert Europe, disciples of Tolstoy and other sects. We who were more intimate together felt no anxiety about the shape the future was to take. Every sect, every faith seemed dead already and of no use. The only duty and destiny we acknowledged was that each one of us should become so completely himself, so utterly faithful to the active seed of nature within him and live in accordance with it that the unknown future should find us prepared and ready for whatever it might bring forth.

For expressed or unexpressed this was clear in our minds, that a new birth and a collapse of the present time was imminent and already discernible. Demian often said to me, "What will come is beyond our powers of imagination. The soul of Europe is an animal which lay fettered for an infinitely long time. When it becomes free, its first impulses will not be the most agreeable. But the ways, straight or crooked, are unimportant provided the real need of the soul – which we have so long and continually drugged and led on false trails – finally comes to light. Then our day will dawn; then we shall be needed, not as leaders or new law-givers – we shall not survive to see the new laws – but rather as men of good will and, as such, ready to go forth and stand prepared wherever fate may need us. Look how all men are ready to accomplish the incredible once their ideals are threatened. But there is no one there when a new ideal, a new and perhaps dangerous and secret stirring of new life is knocking at the door. *We* shall be the handful of people who are there ready to move forward. That is why we are branded – as Cain was – to rouse fear and hatred and drive men out of their unimaginative idyll into more dangerous ways. All men who have striven for the progress of humanity, all of them without exception, were capable and effective only because they were ready to accept their fate. It is true of Moses and Buddha; it is true of Napoleon and Bismarck. What particular movement one serves, what pole one is directed from are matters outside one's own choice. If Bismarck had understood the social democrats and had imposed himself upon them, he would have been a shrewd fellow but hardly a man of destiny. The same applies to Napoleon, Caesar, Loyola, all of them in fact. They must understand their situation biologically and historically. When the upheavals of the earth's surface cast the creatures of the sea on the land and land creatures into the sea, the pre-destined specimens of the various orders were there ready to follow their destiny and accomplished the new and fantastic, and by making new biological adjustments were able to save their species from destruction. We do not know whether these were the same specimens who had previously distinguished themselves among their species as staunch, conservative upholders of the *status quo* or rather as eccentrics and revolutionaries, but we do know that they were ready and could therefore lead their species into the new phase of evolution. Therefore we too intend to be ready."

Frau Eva was often present during these discussions but she herself did not join in. She was a listener and an echo of each one of us as we explained our thoughts, full of confidence and understanding; it seemed as if all our ideas emanated from her and went back to her in the end. It was bliss for me to sit close to her, hear her voice sometimes and share the rich and inspiring atmosphere that surrounded her.

She was immediately aware of any unhappiness or new development within me. I gained the impression that the dreams I had at night were inspired by her. I often recounted them to her and she found them comprehensible and natural; they held no mysteries which she could not grasp intuitively. For a time my dreams followed the pattern of our day-time conversations. I dreamed that the whole world was in a turmoil and that by myself or with Demian I was tensely waiting for the fateful moment. The figure of destiny was veiled but had the features of Frau Eva. To be chosen or rejected by *her*; that was fate.

Often enough she said with a smile, "Your dream is not yet complete, Sinclair. You have forgotten the best part," and then that part would come back to me and I could not understand how I had come to forget it.

At times I was restless and tortured by desire. I thought I could no longer bear to have her near me without taking her in my arms. She soon became aware of this. When on one occasion I absented myself for several days and then returned in a state of distress, she took me aside and said, "You must not give way to desires which you do not believe in. I know what you want. You should however either be capable of renouncing those desires or feel wholly justified in having them. If you are once able to make your request in such a way that you are certain that the fulfilment exists within yourself, then sooner or later the fulfilment will come. But at present you are first wishing, then regretting and full of apprehension. All that must be overcome. Let me tell you a story."

And she told me about a youth who had fallen in love with a star. He stood by the sea, stretched out his arms and prayed to the star, dreamed of it, made it the object of all his thoughts. But he knew, or thought he knew, that a star could not be embraced by a mortal being. He considered it to be his fate to love a star without any hope of fulfilment, and on this conception he founded a poetic philosophy of renunciation, torment and silent suffering that would refine and cleanse him. But all his dreams were directed to the star. Once he stood on the high cliff at night by the sea and contemplated the star and burned with love for it. And in moments of great longing he leaped into space towards the star. But just as he leapt the thought flashed through him, 'this is impossible!' There he lay on the shore, shattered. He had not understood how to love. If at the moment of jumping he had possessed a sure and steadfast faith in the fulfilment of his love he would have soared into the air and have been united with the star . . .

"Love must not entreat," she added, "nor demand. Love must have the power to find its own way to certainty. Then it ceases merely to be attracted and begins to attract. Your love, Sinclair, is attracted by me. When it begins to attract me, I will come. I will not bestow a gift; I must be won."

Another time she told me another story. It concerned a lover whose love was unrequited. He withdrew into his heart and thought his love would consume him. For him the world seemed lost, he no longer saw the blue heaven and the green forest; the brook no longer murmured; he took no pleasure in the sound of the harp; nothing mattered any more, and he had become poor and wretched. But his love increased and he would have welcomed ruin and death rather than renounce possession of this beautiful woman with whom he was infatuated. Then he felt that his passion had burned up everything else inside him and it became so strong and magnetic that the beautiful woman was compelled to follow. She came and he stood with outstretched arms ready to draw her to him. As she stood before him she was completely transformed and he saw that he had won back all he had previously lost. She stood before him and surrendered herself to him and the sky, forest and stream all moved back towards him in new and resplendent colours and spoke to him in his own language. And instead of winning a woman, he had the whole world in his heart and every star in heaven glowed in him and joy coursed through his being. He had loved and by so doing had found himself.

My love for Eva seemed to me to fill my whole life. But every day she looked different. On many occasions I believed that it was not really just her as a person, whom I yearned for with all my being, but that she existed as an outward symbol of my inner self and her sole purpose was to lead me more deeply into myself. Things she said often sounded like replies from my unconscious mind to burning questions which tormented me. There were other moments when as I sat beside her I was consumed with sensual desire and kissed objects which she had touched. And little by little sensual and transcendental love, reality and symbol mingled together. As I thought about her in my room at home in tranquil absorption, I felt her hand in mine and her lips touching my lips. Or I would be conscious of her presence, look into her face, speak with her and hear her voice, not knowing whether she was real or a dream. I began to realize how one can be possessed of a lasting and immortal love. I would gain knowledge of a new religion from my reading, and it would give me the same feeling as a kiss from Eva. She stroked my hair and smiled with all her warm affection, and I had the same feeling as when I took a step forward in knowledge of my inner self. Her person embraced everything that was significant and fateful for me. She could be transformed into each one of my thoughts and each of my thoughts could be transformed into her.

I had been apprehensive about the Christmas vacation which I spent at my parents' home because I thought it was bound to be torture to be away from Eva for two whole weeks. But it did not turn out like that. It was wonderful to be at home and yet be able to think of her. When I arrived back at H—— I stayed away from her for two days in order to savour this security and independence from her physical presence. I had dreams too in which my union with her was consummated in a symbolic act. She was a star and I was a star on my way to her, and we met and mutually attracted, remained together and circled round each other blissfully in all eternity to the accompaniment of the music of the spheres.

I told her this dream on my first visit on returning.

"It is a lovely dream," she said quietly, "Make it true!"

There was a day in early spring that I have never forgotten. I entered the hall; a window was open and a sly current of air wafted the heavy scent of hyacinths through the room. As no one was about, I went upstairs to Max Demian's study. I tapped lightly on the door and as was my custom, went in without waiting for a reply.

The room was dark and all the curtains were drawn. The doors stood open into a small adjoining room where Max had set up a chemical laboratory. From it came the clear white light of the spring sun which shone through the rain clouds. I thought that there was no one in and drew back one of the curtains.

Then I saw Max Demian huddled on a stool by the curtained window, looking strangely different, and it flashed through me that I had already experienced this moment in the past. His arms hung limp, his hands were supported on his knees, his head was slightly bowed over them and his eyes, though open, were unseeing and dead; the pupils reflected a thin thread of light as if they were fragments of glass. His livid face was hollow and expressed nothing but a terrible fixity; he resembled one of those age-old animal masks on a temple gateway. He did not appear to be breathing.

Memory took charge. I had seen him looking exactly

like that once before, may years ago, when I was just a small boy. His eyes had been turned inward in just that way, his hands lay lifeless together, a fly had crawled over his face. And on that occasion – it might have been six years before – he had looked like this, old and timeless; no line in his face today showed any change.

Overcome with fear I quietly left the room and hurried downstairs. I met Eva in the hall. She was pale and seemed tired in a way I had never known her to be before, and just then a shadow passed over the window and the white, dazzling sun suddenly vanished.

"I've been with Max," I whispered gently, "has anything happened? He is asleep or drugged, I don't know which; I saw him look like that once before."

"You didn't wake him up, did you?" she asked quietly.

"No; he didn't hear me. I left the room straight away. Tell me, Frau Eva, what is wrong with him?"

"Don't worry, Sinclair, nothing is wrong. He has withdrawn into himself. It will soon pass."

She stood up and went out into the garden although it was beginning to rain. I felt that she did not want me to accompany her so I walked up and down the hall, inhaled the overpowering scent of the hyacinths, stared at my bird picture above the door and breathed the strange atmosphere of oppressiveness which filled the house that morning. What was it? What had happened?

Frau Eva returned before long. Beads of rain were suspended in her dark hair. She sat down in her armchair. She seemed weary. I approached her, bent over her head and kissed the raindrops out of her hair. Her eyes were bright and calm but the drops tasted like tears.

"Shall I have a look at him?" I whispered.

She gave a weak smile.

"Don't be a child, Sinclair!" she admonished as if she was trying to break a spell in herself. "Go off now and come back later. I can't talk to you just now."

I hurriedly left the house and town and walked in the direction of the mountains with the fine rain slanting against me; low clouds swept by as if they were weighed down with fear. Near the ground there was hardly a breath of wind but a storm seemed to be blowing in higher altitudes. Several times the sun, white and dazzling, momentarily broke through rifts in the steely clouds.

Then a more attractive yellow cloud passed over the sky, piled itself against the other grey bank of cloud and in a few seconds the wind fashioned a shape out of the yellow and blue-grey mass, a gigantic bird that tore itself free from the steel-blue chaos and flew off into the sky with great beats of its wings.

Then a storm became audible and a mixture of hail and rain rattled down. There was a brief, unbelievable and terrifying crack of thunder over the rain-lashed landscape and immediately afterwards a gleam of sunshine burst through, and on the nearby mountains the pale snow shone livid and unreal above the brown forest.

When, hours later, I returned wet through and buffeted by the wind, Demian himself opened the door to me.

He took me up into his room. A gas jet was burning in the laboratory and papers were strewn about the floor. He had evidently been working.

"Sit down," he invited, "you must be exhausted; it was a ghastly storm; it must have been hard going for you out there. There's some tea coming up."

"There's something odd about today," I began hesitantly. "It isn't only this bit of a storm."

He gave me a searching look.

"Did you see anything?"

"Yes; I saw a picture in the clouds, quite clearly for a moment."

"What kind of a picture?"

"A bird."

"The sparrow-hawk? Was it? The bird of your dreams?"

"Yes, it was my sparrow-hawk. Huge and yellow, and it flew off into the steel-blue sky."

Demian heaved a great sigh.

There was a knock. The old servant maid brought in the tea.

"Help yourself, Sinclair – I don't believe it was just chance that you saw the bird."

"Chance? Does one see things like that by chance?"

"Quite right. No. It means something. Do you know what?"

"No; I only feel that it portends a world convulsion of some kind – a move on the part of destiny. Something I believe concerns us all."

He paced up and down.

'A move on the part of destiny?" he shouted, "I dreamed the same kind of thing last night and mother had a premonition yesterday which conveyed the same message ... I dreamed I was climbing up a ladder placed against a tree trunk or tower. When I had reached the top, I saw the whole landscape ablaze – a vast plain with its towns and villages. I can't yet remember it all – it is still somewhat confused."

"Does the dream have any personal message for you?" I asked.

"Of course! No one dreams anything that doesn't concern himself. But it doesn't only concern me; you're quite right. I am pretty accurate in separating the dreams which affect my own soul from the others, rare in all conscience – in which the whole destiny of the human race is involved. I have rarely had such dreams and never before of one of which I could say that it was a prophecy which was fulfilled. The interpretations are too uncertain. But I know for sure that I've dreamed something that doesn't concern me alone. The dream is linked up with other, previous dreams I've had and which it continues. It was those dreams which caused me the forebodings I spoke to you about before. That our world is desperately indolent, we know, but that would be insufficient reason to prophesy its destruction. But for several years I have dreamed dreams which make me feel that the collapse of an old world is imminent. At first these were vague, remote presentiments but they have become increasingly strong and unambiguous. I still know nothing more except that something is going to happen on a vast scale, something terrible in which I personally shall be involved. Sinclair, we shall survive whatever this thing is that we have discussed so often. The world will be renewed. There's a smell of death in the air. Nothing new arises without death. But it is more terrible than I supposed." I stared at him aghast.

"Can't you tell me the rest of your dream?" I ventured to ask him.

He shook his head.

"No."

The door opened and Frau Eva entered.

"So you're sitting here together! You're not feeling sad, children, I hope?"

She looked fresh, all trace of tiredness had vanished. Demian smiled at her and she came up to us like a mother approaching her frightened children.

"Not sad, mother. We have merely been trying to solve the enigma of these new omens. But it doesn't matter. Whatever is to happen will happen suddenly; it will suddenly be there and then we shall learn whatever we need to know."

But I felt depressed, and when I took my leave and walked alone across the hall, the scent of the hyacinths seemed faded, insipid and corpse-like. A shadow had fallen over us.

VIII The Beginning of The End

I had managed to see through the summer term in H——.
We spent nearly all our time in the garden by the river
instead of in the house. The Japanese student, who inci-
dentally had been well and truly defeated in the boxing
match, had departed, the disciple of Tolstoy had gone too.
Demian kept a horse and went for long rides day after
day. I was frequently alone with his mother.

Sometimes I was surprised to find myself living in such
a state of contentment. I had so long been accustomed to
being alone, to living a life of denial, to dragging my
burdens round with me, that these months in H——
seemed like an island of dreams on which I was being
allowed to lead a comfortable and enchanted life among
beautiful and agreeable things. I felt a presentiment that
it was the foretaste of that new, higher companionship
which had been the subject of our speculations. Now and
again I was overwhelmed with a profound regret concerning this happiness, for I knew very well that it could
not last. It was not my lot to breathe freely in fullness and
comfort, I needed the spur of torment. I felt that one day
I would awaken out of these wonderful dream-fantasies
and stand quite alone again, in the cold world of other
people where there was nothing but solitude or struggle
for me.

From now on I stayed close to Frau Eva with feelings
of redoubled affection, glad that my 'fate' still bore those
calm, handsome features.

The summer flashed by easily enough; term was already
nearly over and it would soon be time for farewells. I
dared not think of it; nor did I, but clung to the happy
days like a butterfly to the honey-flower. It had been my

Golden Age, the first fulfilment of my life and my acceptance into a charmed circle – what was to follow? I would have to struggle through again, suffer the old longings, have dreams and live alone.

One day this foreboding came over me with such force that my love for Eva flared up suddenly and caused me great pain. My God, what a short time I had left; soon I should no longer be seeing her, no longer hearing her good, assured step about the house, no longer finding her flowers on my table! And what had I achieved? I had luxuriated in dreams and comfort instead of winning her, instead of struggling for her and clasping her to me for ever! Everything she had told me about true love came back to me, a hundred stirring, admonitory messages, and as many gentle promises and words of encouragement, too, perhaps; and what had I made out of it all? Nothing.

I stood in the middle of the room, summoned my whole conscious being and thought of Eva. I wanted to gather all the power of my soul in order to make her aware of my love and attract her to me. She must come; she must long for my embrace, my kisses must tremble on her ripe lips.

I stood and concentrated every effort until I grew cold from my fingers and feet inwards. I felt the strength ebbing out of me. For a few moments something inside me seemed to contract – something bright and cold; for a second it was as though I had a crystal of glass in my heart, and I knew that it was myself. The chill crept up to my chest.

When I woke up from this terrible tenseness, I felt that something was happening. I was mortally tired but ready to see Eva come into my room, glowing and ecstatic.

The trample of horses' hooves could now be heard down in the street, the metallic sound drew near, then suddenly stopped. I leaped to the window, and saw Demian dismounting below. I ran down.

"What's happened, Demian? Nothing wrong with your mother, I hope?"

He did not hear my words. He was very pale, and the perspiration was running down his cheeks from both sides of his forehead. He tied the bridle of his sweating horse to the garden fence, gripped my arm and walked down the street with me.

"Do you know what?"

I did not know anything.

Demian squeezed my arm and turned his face towards me with a strange, sombre look of sympathy.

"Yes, young 'un; it's started now. You knew about the strained relations between ourselves and Russia . . ."

"What? Is it war? I've never believed it possible."

He spoke in a whisper although nobody was anywhere near.

"It hasn't been declared but it *is* war, you may be sure of that. I didn't worry you about it before, but since then I've come across new signs on three occasions. It's not going to be the end of the world, an earthquake or revolution, but war. You will see the effect on people. They will acclaim it with enthusiasm; everybody is already looking forward to the first onslaught – so dull have their lives become. But you will see, Sinclair; this is only the beginning. Perhaps it will be a great war, a very great war. The new world is beginning and the new world will be terrible for those who cling to the old. What will *you* do?"

I was dumbfounded, so strange and impossible did it sound.

"I don't know – and what about you?"

He shrugged his shoulders.

"An immediate mobilization has been ordered. I've been recalled. I'm a lieutenant."

"You! I hadn't any idea!"

"Yes. It was one of the things on which I compromised. You know how I hate to attract attention and have always erred on the side of being over-correct. I believe I shall be at the Front within a week."

"For God's sake . . ."

"Now, young 'un, you mustn't get sentimental about it. It won't give me any pleasure to order men to fire at living targets, but that will be merely incidental. Each one of us will be caught up in the great wheel. You too. You'll certainly be called up."

"And what about your mother, Demian?"

Now, for the first time my thoughts turned back to what had been taking place a quarter of an hour before. How the world had changed! I had been summoning all my strength to conjure up the rarest image and now fate was suddenly standing staring at me from a grimly threatening mask.

"My mother? Oh, we don't need to have any anxiety about her. She's safe, safer than anyone else in the world. Do you love her as much as all that?"

"You knew it then, Demian?"

He laughed a cheerful, unconstrained laugh.

"Little boy! Of course I knew! No one has ever called my mother 'Frau Eva' without loving her. How did it happen? You sent a message either to me or to her today, didn't you?"

"Yes, I . . . did appeal . . . I appealed to Frau Eva."

"She was aware of it. She suddenly sent me away. I must go to you. I had just been telling her the news about Russia."

We turned back and did not say much more; he untied his horse and mounted.

It was in my room upstairs that I first realized how much Demian's news, and still more the previous strain, had exhausted me. But Frau Eva had heard me. I had conveyed the message of my heart. She would have come herself – if – but how strange it all was and how fundamentally beautiful. Now there was to be a war, and what we had so often talked about was to take place. Demian had known so much about it beforehand. How strange that the stream of the world would no longer be flowing just vaguely somewhere – it would suddenly flow right through our hearts. How strange that wild and fateful adventure was calling us and that now or very soon the moment had come when the world needed us, when it would be tranformed. Demian was right; we should not sentimentalize the situation. The only remarkable thing was that I was now to share my lonely 'fate' with so many other men, with the whole world, in fact. So much the better!

I was prepared. When I walked through the town during the evening, every street corner was buzzing with great excitement. The word 'war' was on everybody's lips.

I went to Frau Eva's; we ate supper in the summerhouse. I was the only guest. No one said a word about the war. Only later on, shortly before my departure, Eva said, "Dear Sinclair, you appealed to me today. You know why I didn't come to you myself . . . But don't forget; you know how to get a message to me now; and whenever you need someone who bears the 'sign' you can appeal to me again."

She rose to her feet and preceded me into the garden twilight. Tall and queenly, the woman of mystery strolled among the silent trees and above her head the myriad stars glowed tenderly.

I am coming to the end of my story. Events ran their rapid course. The war came soon and Demian, wonderfully strange in his uniform with his silver-grey cloak, left us. I accompanied his mother home. Soon I too took my leave of her. She kissed me on the lips and clasped me for a moment to her breast, and her large eyes burned closely and steadfastly into mine.

All men became as brothers. They thought it was patriotism and honour, but it was destiny into whose unveiled face they were all momentarily allowed to glance. Young men left their barracks, entrained, and on many faces I could read a 'sign' – not ours but a noble and worthy sign that meant devotion and death. I too was embraced by men whom I had never seen before and I understood and gladly responded. It was a kind of intoxication that, it had nothing to do with the will of destiny, but it was a noble intoxication and moving because they had all stared into the eyes of fate for that brief, revealing moment.

It was nearly winter already when I was drafted to the Front. To start with, despite the excitement of being under fire for the first time, I was disillusioned. Formerly I had pondered much on why man was capable of living for an ideal on so few occasions. Now I saw that many, indeed, all men were capable of dying for an ideal. Only they had no use for a free, self-chosen ideal; it must be shared and accepted.

As time went on, however, I saw that I had under-estimated humanity.

However much service and common danger ironed them out, I saw many men, living and dying, approach the will of fate with great dignity . . . Many, very many, wore not only during battle but at every moment of the day, the distant, resolute, as it were fanatic look in their eyes which knows nothing of aims, and signifies complete absorption in the horror of the moment. Whatever they might believe or think, they were ready, expendable, from them the future would be shaped . . . And the more the eyes of the world were focused on war, heroism, honour and all the old ideals, the more remote and increasingly improbable sounded any whisper of apparent humanity; and yet all this was only on the surface, in the way the question of foreign and political aims of the war remained superficial. Deep down underneath something was taking shape. Something akin to a new humanity. For I could see many – and many died by my side – who were aware that hatred and rage, slaughter and annihilation were not bound up with the real, ultimate aims. No, the objectives like the goals were quite fortuitous. Their most primitive, even their wildest feelings were not for the enemy; their bloody task was merely an outward radiation of the inner soul, the divided soul filled with the lust to rage and kill, annihilate and die so that it might be born anew. A giant bird was struggling out of the egg; the egg was the world and the world must first be rent asunder.

One night in early spring I was standing in front of a farm which we had occupied. A slight wind was blowing in fitful gusts; over the high Flanders sky rode armies of clouds with a hint of moon somewhere behind them. I had felt uneasy the whole day, tormented by vague fears. Now as I stood on guard in the darkness, I pondered deeply on the people who had figured in my life. Frau Eva, Demian. I stood leaning against a poplar tree; staring into the scurrying clouds where lurking drifts of brightness were quickly transformed into large swelling phantasmagoric shapes. I could feel by the strange weakness of my pulse, the insensitivity of my skin to the wind and rain, the readiness of my inner responses that a guide and leader was not far away from me.

A great town could be seen in the clouds and out of it poured millions of men who spread in hosts over vast landscapes. In their midst strode a mighty, godlike form with shining stars in her hair, as huge as a mountain but having the features of Frau Eva. The ranks of men were swallowed up into her as into a gigantic cave and vanished from sight. The goddess crouched on the ground, the 'sign' shone on her brow. She seemed to be in the grip of a dream. She closed her eyes and her great countenance was twisted in pain. Suddenly she called out, and from her forehead sprang stars, many thousands of them which leaped in graceful curves across the dark heavens.

One of the stars shot straight towards me with a clear,

ringing sound; it seemed to be seeking me out. Then it burst with a roar into a thousand sparks, bore me aloft and cast me down to the ground again; the world was shattered above me with a thunderous roar . . .

They found me near the poplar covered with earth and with many wounds.

I lay in a cellar, shells roared over me. I lay in a waggon and staggered across devastated fields. Mostly I slept and was unconscious. But the more deeply I slept, the more strongly I felt that someone was drawing me onwards, that I was held in tow by some force that had mastery over me.

I lay in a stable on straw; it was dark. Someone had trodden on my hand. But my inner self still pressed forward and I was drawn on more forcefully than ever. Again I lay on a waggon and later on a stretcher or a ladder. More urgently than ever I felt I was being summoned somewhere and that I must finally get there.

Now I was at my goal. It was night; I was fully conscious. I had just felt an irresistible inner urge. Now I lay in a room, in a bed on the floor and knew that I had reached the place where I had been summoned. I glanced around me. There was another mattress close to mine occupied by someone who now bent forward to look at me. He had the 'sign' on his forehead. It was Demian . . .

I could not speak and he either could not or did not want to. He was content to look at me. The light from a lamp hung above him on the wall played on his face. He smiled at me.

He gazed into my eyes for what seemed an infinity of time. Slowly he edged his face nearer to mine until we were almost touching one another.

"Sinclair!" he whispered.

I indicated with a glance that I understood him. He smiled again, almost as if in sympathy.

"Young 'un," he said with a smile.

His lips were now quite close to mine. Quietly he continued to speak.

"Can you still remember Franz Kromer?" he asked. I blinked my assent and even managed to smile.

"Listen, young Sinclair, I've got to go. Perhaps you'll need my help against Kromer or something else ... If you send a message I shan't come riding crudely on horseback or by railway train next time. You'll have to listen to your inner voice and then you will hear me speak within you. Do you understand? And there is something else. Frau Eva said that if things ever went badly with you, I was to pass on a kiss from her which she gave me ... Close your eyes, Sinclair."

I closed my eyes in obedience. I felt the brush of a kiss on my lips on which there was a bead of blood that never seemed to diminish. Then I fell asleep.

Next morning they woke me up; I had to have my wounds dressed. When I was finally properly awake I turned quickly towards the mattress next to mine. A stranger lay on it whom I had never seen before.

The dressing was a painful business. So was everything else that happened to me afterwards. But when on the many such occasions I find the key and look deep down into myself where the images of destiny lie slumbering in the dark mirror, I only need to bend my head over the black mirror to see my own image which now wholly resembles him, my friend and leader.

The world's greatest novelists now available in Triad/Panther Books

Aldous Huxley

Brave New World	£1.95	☐
Island	£1.95	☐
After Many a Summer	£1.95	☐
Brief Candles	£1.95	☐
The Devils of Loudun	£1.95	☐
Eyeless in Gaza	£2.50	☐
Antic Hay	£1.95	☐
Crome Yellow	£1.50	☐
Point Counter Point	£1.95	☐
Those Barren Leaves	£1.95	☐
The Genius and the Goddess	£1.95	☐
Time Must Have a Stop	£2.50	☐
The Doors of Perception/		
Heaven and Hell (non-fiction)	£1.95	☐
The Human Situation (non-fiction)	£1.95	☐
Grey Eminence (non-fiction)	£1.95	☐
Brave New World Revisited (non-fiction)	£1.95	☐
The Gioconda Smile and other stories	£2.50	☐
Ape and Essence	£1.95	☐

Hermann Hesse

Stories of Five Decades	£2.50	☐
Journey to the East	£1.95	☐
Demian	£1.95	☐
Pictor's Metamorphoses	£1.95	☐
My Belief (non-fiction)	£1.25	☐
Reflections (non-fiction)	95p	☐
Hermann Hesse: A Pictorial Biography	£1.50	☐

To order direct from the publisher just tick the titles you want
and fill in the order form.

The world's greatest novelists now available in Triad/Panther Books

Ernest Hemingway

The Old Man and The Sea	
Fiesta	
For Whom the Bell Tolls	£1.50 ☐
A Farewell to Arms	£1.95 ☐
The Snows of Kilimanjaro	£2.50 ☐
The Essential Hemingway	£1.95 ☐
To Have and Have Not	£1.95 ☐
Green Hills of Africa	£2.95 ☐
Men Without Women	£1.95 ☐
A Moveable Feast	£2.50 ☐
The Torrents of Spring	£2.50 ☐
Across the River and Into the Trees	£1.95 ☐
Winner Take Nothing	£2.50 ☐
The Fifth Column	£1.95 ☐
Death in the Afternoon (non-fiction)	£1.95 ☐

Richard Hughes

A High Wind in Jamaica	£1.95 ☐
In Hazard	£2.95 ☐
Fox in the Attic	£1.25 ☐
The Wooden Shepherdess	£1.50 ☐

James Joyce

Dubliners	£1.50 ☐
A Portrait of the Artist as a Young Man	£1.50 ☐
Stephen Hero	£1.95 ☐
The Essential James Joyce	£1.95 ☐
Exiles (play)	£1.95 ☐
	£2.95 ☐
	£1.25 ☐

To order direct from the publisher just tick the titles you want and fill in the order form.

The world's greatest novelists now available in Panther Books

Simon Raven
'Alms for Oblivion' series

Fielding Gray	£1.95	☐
Sound the Retreat	£1.95	☐
The Sabre Squadron	£1.95	☐
The Rich Pay Late	£1.95	☐
Friends in Low Places	£1.95	☐
The Judas Boy	£1.95	☐
Places Where They Sing	£1.95	☐
Come Like Shadows	£2.50	☐
Bring Forth the Body	£1.95	☐
The Survivors	£1.95	☐

Other Titles

The Roses of Picardie	£1.50	☐
The Feathers of Death	35p	☐
Doctors Wear Scarlet	30p	☐

Paul Scott
The Raj Quartet

The Jewel in the Crown	£2.95	☐
The Day of the Scorpion	£2.95	☐
The Towers of Silence	£2.95	☐
A Division of the Spoils	£2.95	☐

Other Titles

The Bender	£1.95	☐
The Corrida at San Feliu	£2.50	☐
A Male Child	£1.50	☐
The Alien Sky	£2.50	☐
The Chinese Love Pavilion	£2.50	☐
The Mark of the Warrior	£1.95	☐
Johnnie Sahib	£2.50	☐
The Birds of Paradise	£1.50	☐
Staying On	£1.95	☐

To order direct from the publisher just tick the titles you want and fill in the order form.

All these books are available at your local bookshop or newsagent, or can be ordered direct from the publisher..

To order direct from the publisher just tick the titles you want and fill in the form below.

Name _____

Address _____

_____

Send to:
Panther Cash Sales
PO Box 11, Falmouth, Cornwall TR10 9EN.

Please enclose remittance to the value of the cover price plus:

UK 45p for the first book, 20p for the second book plus 14p per copy for each additional book ordered to a maximum charge of £1.63.

BFPO and Eire 45p for the first book, 20p for the second book plus 14p per copy for the next 7 books, thereafter 8p per book.

Overseas 75p for the first book and 21p for each additional book.

Panther Books reserve the right to show new retail prices on covers, which may differ from those previously advertised in the text or elsewhere.